The
Other
One

The Other One

stories

HASANTHIKA SIRISENA

University of Massachusetts Press
Amherst and Boston

ISBN 978-1-62534-218-8 (alk. pbk)

Designed by Sally Nichols
Set in ArnhemFine
Printed and bound by Maple Press, Inc.

Library of Congress Cataloging-in-Publication Data
A catalog record for this book is available from the Library of Congress.

British Library Cataloguing-in-Publication Data
A catalogue record for this book is available from the British Library.

For Neela and Leo

CONTENTS

The
Other
One

Third Country National

Anura tended the aquarium in the airbase DFAC. It wasn't his true job, but he had volunteered and was responsible for whatever happened. So he felt slightly ill when he noticed the puffer fish, the newest addition, idling listlessly in the corner of the tank. That puffer fish had arrived along with a recent shipment of aquarium rocks and plants. The first day, the fish sputtered in the water, unable to swim because of a mutilated fin and tail. A few days later, red dots appeared on the fish's belly, then white protrusions. Anura noticed a wound, fleshy and raw. He was not to blame for the sick fish, he was sure, but his boss might not agree. Sometimes she was fair, but many times, especially when she'd been fighting with her own boss, she took it out on the TCNs.

The 55-gallon, salt-water glass aquarium belonged to the United States Military and was situated on a console at the far end of an airbase mess hall. The airbase was located in Kuwait, and its DFAC was nothing more than a large, trailer: mustard yellow aluminum siding on the outside, faux wood paneling on the inside. The interior had been decorated in red, white and blue: red and white streamers hung from the ceiling as if the place were trapped in perpetual party mode, blue roman shades on the windows, red plastic tablecloths covered the dining tables. On one wall hung a flat screen television always turned to

CNN; vending machines offering bags of peanuts, soda, and non-alcoholic beer lined the opposite wall. Laminated posters had been taped to the wood paneling. Anura could not read English so, every food service, his friend and fellow TCN Ibrahim read the signs for Anura. Donuts. Ice Cream. Cheeseburgers. General Tso's Chicken. Anura would at least be able to remain well fed if, as he hoped, he ever made it to Canada. The airbase kept the DFAC open most of the day and late into the evenings, and the soldiers came and went as they pleased. The fish tank was—after CNN—the biggest draw. Some of the soldiers came and sat in front of it, staring at the fish as they slowly chewed their meals. Anura understood why they came. He spent any free time—and there was very little given to him—watching the tank and caring for it. It calmed Anura and helped him forget.

When Anura first encountered the aquarium, emerald green patches of algae streaked its glass. The last TCN in charge of it had left a few days before and no one had yet been assigned to tank duty. Anura cleaned the filter, fixed the pH level, and took on the tank's care, even though he hadn't had to, because he had always been enthralled by aquariums and because this tank in particular amazed him, gave him hope. The military had brought this fish tank to the Kuwaiti desert—a desert without a single drop of naturally occurring water and certainly no naturally occurring fish—to ensure its people did not forget America's power. It was a sign of how the American military, unlike the Sri Lanka military, paid attention to the minutest details of its soldiers' lives. This was why America was so powerful and Sri Lanka was nothing more than a small, useless island, slowly choking itself.

Anura took off his garrison cap and tucked it neatly into the pocket of his chef pants. He moved closer to the tank, put his fingers to the glass.

"Ich."

Anura jumped. He hadn't realized someone was standing behind him. When he turned, he found a young man—tall and olive complexioned—wearing camouflage combat fatigues, and a young woman—a blond who, despite pockmarked skin was very pretty—also in

2

fatigues. Soldiers didn't speak to Anura, and he felt shy to have drawn the attention of these two.

"That's not nice," the girl said. She made a moue at her friend and beamed a sincere, unabashed adoration. "I think it's a very nice tank."

The soldier folded his arms across his chest and scowled. "I don't mean *ick,*" he insisted. "I mean *ich*. It's a disease. Fish get it."

Anura shook his head. "No, not ich." He pointed to the ailing fish. "You must look."

The soldier leaned in close. His breath formed, against the glass, a thin fog that dissolved on contact and then, a few seconds later, reappeared. The soldier was undoubtedly handsome: square jaw, dark eyes, broad and muscular. Three months ago, when Anura first arrived on the base, he would have guessed the boy to be an American Black but Ibrahim had warned him not to jump to such conclusions. "These Americans, they can tell each other apart, but you cannot," he had warned. "You make an A-S-S out of yourself, when you *assume*." It had taken weeks for Anura to figure out what the letters A-S-S stood for.

The soldier shook his head. "I don't see it," he muttered.

"Worms," Anura offered solemnly. Both soldiers grimaced. "I take sick fish. Pull worm, one by one with—" Anura formed a pincer with his thumb and index finger.

"Tweezers." The male soldier nodded approvingly. "You know about fish tanks."

Anura looked down at the ground and feigned humility though he was deeply pleased the boy had noticed. "I take care of aquarium at Cinnamon Grand in Colombo."

"You can't give it medicine?" the girl demanded. "They give dogs worm medicine."

Anura sighed. "I not find right medicine here."

"You need Dimilin. I remember that much," the male soldier said. He looked over at the girl. "I used to own a fish tank."

"Dimilin, yes," said Anura though he didn't know what Dimilin was. The soldier looked so earnest and Anura wanted to trust him.

Suddenly, the girl soldier tapped the glass. Anura began to tell her

3

politely to stop, but her friend grabbed her hand and yanked it back. "Are you trying to scare the fish?"

"I just saw the most beautiful creature. But it wasn't a fish."

"Only fish and snails in tank, madam," Anura said.

"I'm pretty sure this was something else. It had legs. Fish and snails don't have legs." She peered up at her friend. "But it was pretty. Like a rainbow. And it glowed."

Anura and the soldier boy gaped at her. "What have you been smoking?" the male soldier demanded.

The girl didn't answer. She gave an exaggerated pout and, as both Anura and her friend watched, sashayed away.

Anura's regular job on the base was to clean: the TCNs in his unit rotated between cleaning the DFAC, the living quarters, and the latrines. The base officially belonged to the Air Force but it was also a way station: a transition point where military units stopped on their way to Iraq and Afghanistan. The base received Marines, Army, Navy and Air Force as well as RAF; none stayed longer than a few days. Outside contractors ran most airbase operations including the DFAC and the septic system. The average Kuwaiti was too wealthy to work on a military base so the outside contractors hired mostly third country nationals, like Anura, to do the cleaning, cooking, and maintenance.

Ibrahim feared the soldiers. Anura couldn't tell them apart to fear them. Ibrahim said the soldiers hated the TCNs, called them names—hajis, and other things. Anura suspected most of the soldiers looked right through the TCNs and never saw them at all. It was some solace Ibrahim needed, to believe he mattered enough. Truth was they didn't.

Experience had taught Anura real, unadulterated hate rarely served as an adequate explanation for people's behavior. Yes, hate existed but not to the degree he'd once thought. He had worked for other soldiers once, for soldiers in the Sri Lanka army near Jaffna and then later near Ampara. Those Sri Lanka soldiers had fought because the government

4

promised their families clay floors, because the government had promised land and money. He didn't know why the Americans and the British fought but these child soldiers (they were after all only seventeen, eighteen, nineteen—Anura had a son nearly their age) with their broad, ruddy faces were most of them too naïve and self-absorbed, too deeply cocooned and cosseted by their iPod worlds, to hate. It seemed to him all the horror he'd seen, and he'd seen great evil, happened because a soldier's behavior was predictable the way a little child's behavior was predictable. All these soldiers spoke and felt and acted the way Anura's children had once spoken and felt and done, because that was what the other children were speaking, feeling, and acting, because following the others was the only way any of their actions made sense. Anura felt sorry for the soldiers on the base, as he had the Sri Lankan soldiers, but, unlike Ibrahim, he never feared them.

<hr>

The next evening, after his shift was over, Anura scooped out some salt water from the tank and netted the puffer fish. It hadn't been hard; the fish didn't struggle. Anura found the brightest spot in the DFAC and hunched over the bowl.

The sick fish listed in the water. Anura didn't even have to hold it still. With tweezers commandeered by Ibrahim, Anura pulled at one of the tiny, pale protrusions. What came out was clear and slim and wrestled to free itself. Anura squeezed the tips of the tweezers together. How easy to erase a living thing from this world.

He'd nearly finished when the two soldiers from the other evening slid onto the bench across from him. Under the bright light, Anura could see that both of them were older than he'd originally thought, maybe in their mid-twenties.

"Is it going to be okay?" the male soldier asked.

Anura frowned. "I don't know." He counted the letters stitched on the pocket of the soldier's combat jacket. Six. Ibrahim had taught him this meant either U.S. Army or Navy. "You are what kind of soldiers?"

"Lieutenants. I'm a translator." He pointed at the woman. "And she's an expert on," he raised an eyebrows, "Arab thinking."

The girl soldier held out her hand. "Diana. Pleasure to meet you."

Anura took the hand and shook it lightly.

The other soldier held out his hand also. "Khan." Anura blinked at him. The lieutenant gave a weak smile. "My mom's Pakistani. My dad's a Star Trek fan."

Under the bright light, Anura saw how scarred Diana's face was: little raw, crimson pustules dotted her cheeks and forehead. But she had wide green eyes and the thin, sweet smile of someone who found very little funny but tried to laugh anyway. He was struck again by how essentially pretty she was. "You are Arab?" he asked. "You do not look Arab."

"No baby. Puerto Rican. Born and bred."

Khan jabbed a finger at her. "She's a fucking genius at language. She can spend a week in a country and speak the language fluently." A blush crept across Diana's face. "Say something to her. In your language."

Anura smiled shyly. "Oya hari lassana."

She cocked her head to the side and wrinkled her nose. "Thank you."

Anura jerked his head back. "How you know what I say? You speak Sinhala?"

She winked. "I'm a psychologist. And you seem like a nice guy."

"Translators? So you do not fight?" Anura asked them.

Diana shook her head. "No, we tell the big guns what to do. Four years at John Jay and two years at NYU, and I fucking get to tell the generals what to do."

In the bowl, the fish began to thrash about. The tale and the uninjured fin quivered. It opened its mouth wide; the gills fanned exposing the pink flesh beneath. It struggled to right itself.

"Look. It's getting better," said Khan.

But Anura stared. When he didn't look up, when he didn't agree, Khan and Diana quieted also. They had seen it before too, Anura knew.

That last spark, that last instinctual push for life, before the end. They all stared at the bowl silently.

— ·—···· —

Anura had gotten this job in Kuwait because he could speak English. He'd been working at the Cinnamon Grand in Colombo for nearly three years. He had slept tucked behind an industrial dryer in the laundry facility and sent what money he earned to his family. The fat, balding man in sunglasses had approached him one morning in the dining room. The man was Sinhalese, Anura could tell, but spoke with a posh British accent. He was looking for experienced hotel workers for a luxury hotel in Kuwait. Anura had heard the stories, but he didn't ask questions. He needed to leave Sri Lanka—he was tired of hiding in the laundry room—and it no longer mattered to him much if he lived or died.

Still, when the smuggler took his passport from him—for safe-keeping he claimed—Anura experienced fear. At the airbase, his boss, a very beautiful black woman, returned Anura's passport and handed him a three-page contract. She demanded he sign. The contract was in English. When he hesitated, she gave an annoyed sigh. "These are your rights and privileges," she drawled. "It also states your salary." Anura pretended to peruse it and then carefully wrote his name, the only written English he knew, in neat block letters.

Anura's new home was a tent. It housed twelve other TCNs: four from Sri Lanka, three from Nepal, one from Nigeria, three from India, one from Bangladesh. The space was littered with dirty laundry, empty bottles of coconut oil, tubes of Sesa hair gel, wrappers—Gold Leaf cig-arettes, Crunchie bars, McDonald's—spent prepaid cell phones and phone cards, bottles of arrack—smuggled in because it was impos-sible to buy alcohol in Kuwait without a government-granted ration card. The legs and metal runners of the cots were sticky and glistening, coated with petroleum jelly to ward off bed bugs. Anura had one morn-ing sat down on his cot in his chef uniform trousers and had sported,

7

for the rest of the day, two long, greasy streaks just below the backs of his knees. The air reeked of curry and sweat and the rank musk of adult men. At first, Anura had been afraid of being robbed as he slept. But he soon learned there was an implicit order to his comrades' relations. They didn't touch each other's belongings. They maintained a formal distance unless befriended.

Ibrahim, a fellow Sri Lankan, slept in the cot beside Anura's. On Anura's first evening, Ibrahim explained things were not all that bad on the airbase. "They could have sent you to Iraq, machan. People get killed there. Nobody gets killed here. Not unless he gets hit by a sharif's limousine while crossing the highway to the Burger King." Ibrahim sat up on his cot and swung his legs over the side. He was tall and rangy. He had a cadaverous face—hollowed out eye sockets and cheeks. Anura found it painful to focus on Ibrahim's gaunt face too long. His gaze drifted to a corner of the tent. Ibrahim stretched his legs across the gap between the two cots and propped his feet on the middle of Anura's mattress. "Fifty square feet of personal space. That's what the contract promises." He giggled. "I guess that means I have very long legs."

A month later, when Anura received his first paycheck, he stared at the row of curlicues, dots, and slashes unable to decipher any of it. On the next paycheck, he was paid a different amount, a larger amount. And a different amount the next time. When he asked, Ibrahim smirked and replied in English. "Who the fuck knows? Truth is they could do anything they want to us. No one knows. No one cares. We're lucky to be paid at all."

⸺

The next day, when Anura peered into the tank, he noticed two of the angelfish and one of the clownfish had disappeared. There were supposed to be seven, but he counted five. Anura opened the lid and scanned the surface of the water. It was clear, no floaters.

After his shift, he stood in front of the tank, hoping the missing fish would reappear. He studied the plants. Nothing. He searched deep into the plastic castle, but that was the catfish's abode, no other fish went near. The remaining fish darted to the surface; they opened their mouths expectantly. Anura dropped a pinch of fish flakes into the tank and re-counted.

Khan and Diana sidled next to him. "What's wrong now?" Khan asked.

"Fish are missing. There must be seven angelfish and two clownfish."

Diana counted. She stopped, confused, and started counting again. "Maybe they're hiding."

"They no hide from food," Anura said. He walked around to the side of the tank. "And many snails here yesterday."

"So they're dead?" asked Khan.

"But no bodies."

They all three of them stood, the only sound the low buzz of news being broadcast on the flat screen television behind them. Diana jumped up. "There," she pointed to the edge of the tank. "I'm not crazy. There's the thing I saw."

Anura walked back around. "Right there." Anura followed her line of sight and saw the creature. It was over three inches long. A gray, segmented carapace protected its body; the head and legs that peeked out from underneath were brightly colored, magenta and yellow and emerald green. It scurried across the rocks toward the snails, brandished a fluorescent green claw, and knocked a single snail off the glass.

"Fuck, what is it?" cried Khan.

Anura shivered.

"It's beautiful," whispered Diana. The creature dragged the snail across the rocks.

Diana nodded at Anura. "You don't know what it is?"

Anura shook his head. It looked like a shrimp but was too colorful. He'd never seen anything like it. Anura gulped.

Diana shoved her hand into the pocket of her combat fatigues and pulled out a cell phone. She flipped the phone open, held it to the glass, and clicked. As she did, the creature clutched the snail between its legs, flipped its hind legs into the air, twirled balletically, and slid into a hole in the gravel.

"Got it." Diana held out the phone to the others. There was a picture of the thing, fuzzy but unmistakable. "Give me a couple of hours. I'll find out what it is."

"It's a mantis shrimp. They can be sometimes accidentally transported into a tank," Diana told Anura the next morning. "And they can be a big pain in the ass. That's what's eating the other fish. You have to get it out."

All three—Anura, Diana, and Khan—walked over to the aquarium together. Anura counted only two remaining angelfish. "It's going to keep picking off the fish," said Khan. "Unless you do something."

"Yeah but be careful," warned Diana. "Those claws can cause major ass damage. Crush a finger. They've been known to break a glass tank." Anura stared at her. He, Khan, and Diana had formed some strange camaraderie, but he really didn't understand why. They saw something in him he didn't. Or, more precisely, they saw something in him that wasn't there. They'd realize their mistake soon.

When Anura explained to the boss that he should take an hour or two and empty the tank, the boss hadn't even looked up from her paperwork. "If you need more things to do, we can give you a double-shift cleaning latrines."

Later that evening, Anura took the fishnet and opened the lid of the tank. The thick scent of salt, and fish, and algae nearly sent Anura reeling back, as it did every time he cleaned the tank. He pinched his nose and thrust his arm into the tank water. The remaining fish zipped behind the plants. The water felt unnaturally warm and slimy but he persisted. With the net, Anura began digging in the rocks. He kept digging slowly and carefully for nearly an hour, even as his arm began to go numb with the effort. Nothing.

Anura walked to the kitchen and carefully washed away the salt and scum. When he returned to the tank, only one angelfish remained.

The mantis shrimp snaked out from the rocks. It danced for Anura. Its glowing appendages twirled as it jigged from side to side. Its claws thrust forward in salute. Watching it, Anura's stomach churned. He hated this creature. Diana had called it beautiful, but Anura could barely stand to look at it. This thing was not just destroying the tank by itself, Anura was sure he had himself somehow created it. It was a result of his karma, all he'd done—and hadn't done—reified. It had come because of him. It had come for him.

As Anura watched, the mantis shrimp bobbed to the corner. There something—some movement, some trick of the light—caught its attention and caused the creature to bristle. It brandished a claw and struck the side of the tank, hard. Surprised, Anura stepped back. The mantis shrimp raised its claw to strike again. Anura tapped the glass. The mantis shrimp reared and scurried underneath the rocks.

A man can escape only so many times. Anura had already escaped twice: once from Sri Lanka to Kuwait and once from the army fort in Ampara. He'd been a cook there for the third battalion Sinha regiment. Not that there was much to cook. The troops and the police stationed at the fort got by on one meal a day: rice, dhal, and dried sprats. On a lucky day, they received a shipment of soya meat. Still, Anura had been a good cook and the man in charge of the camp, Brigadier Commander Peiris, treated Anura well.

There was a stray camp dog—a mutt with the head of a retriever, the chest and stomach of a beagle and the rear end of an Alsatian. Anura befriended it. At first, the camp dog had refused to eat the soya meat and Peiris had been impressed by the dog's choosiness. Out here in the jungle, in the middle of a war, and the dog could be a snob. He must be a Kandyan king reborn. Anura had explained that Peiris only had to wait. The dog was only being coy; seeing if it could do better. Finally it would give up and settle. As Anura predicted, after two days of refusing the dog ate a plate of idiyappam. Peiris had been impressed with Anura after that, called him a wise man and a good judge of character.

When they first arrived at the fort, the soldiers had carried their .303 rifles everywhere, even to eat. Anura had trained himself to fall asleep quickly, during a lull in the shelling. Once asleep, no amount of mortar rounds woke him. He had learned that about himself and felt proud of his fortitude. He might not have minded going on at the fort. He put up with it for many months. But in the last two weeks the shelling had ended, and the snipers disappeared. A rumor went around the camp that Prabhakaran had ordered an LTTE pullout. There was even idle talk the Sinha regiment would be sent back to Colombo.

The day of the raid, the troops were in a good mood. Some of the soldiers had been given leave to see Damith Fonseka and Anoja Weerasinghe the next day, and they would be leaving soon. The two actors were performing at the base in Batticaloa. The soldiers hadn't seen a television for the past year; now these actors were arriving to entertain them. Anura, of course, couldn't go. Who would cook for those forced to remain behind?

It was early afternoon. Anura was finishing his lunch. Peiris had come to the kitchen for his daily cup of tea. Anura scraped a portion of his meal into the camp dog's dish. Peiris watched him do this with a smile. Anura's kindness to the animal, Peiris told him, would earn him much merit for the next life.

The two of them heard the dull roaring first. Peiris straightened and peered out, concerned. But he didn't move. Then came the whoosh of mortar rounds and the thud as they hit the ground. The yelling and screaming began. Anura and Peiris ran out of the kitchen.

Anura stopped short as mortar rounds hit the ground in front of him, killing a few of the soldiers still lolling in the eating area. The roaring grew louder and then something large, metal, solid, hit the side of the fort with a crunch. One of the mud walls gave way and an armor-plated bucket loader trundled over the rubble. As Anura stood petrified, the LTTE fighters positioned ladders on the walls that remained. Their men began scaling. Anura saw Peiris ahead waving his arms and ordering his men and the police. One of the soldiers raised his rifle and aimed at a fighter who had reached the top. Suddenly, the Sinha regiment soldier spun around. Seconds later, his head burst, a pulp of red, brown and black. Anura heard a popping—like Chinese firecrackers—and the ground around him became animate—dirt and moss and rocks flying into the air. Pebbles nicked at Anura's face and arms. Anura didn't wait to see any more. He and the camp dog ran into a clutch of hibiscus bushes at the far end of the fort.

Anura didn't know how long the fighting lasted. It was still light when the gunfire stopped. He peeked out from underneath the bush where he was hiding. The ground exuded smoke as if it had been set afire. A burnt smell of gunpowder and seared flesh hung heavy. As Anura watched from his hiding place, an LTTE commander lined up the soldiers and police who were still alive. He and his men shot them one by one. Anura watched the men he'd fed and joked with fall to the ground. Some seemed to die quickly. Others convulsed for what seemed to Anura like minutes. One of those executed toward the end, when the LTTE fighters were becoming tired and careless, skittered in the dirt before having to be shot a second and a third time. Once they were done, the fighters set the corpses on fire. The only man they didn't kill was Peiris. They bound him and led him out of the fort with them. Peiris walked hunched over, his head drooping so severely his chin rested against his chest. He dragged his right leg behind him and could barely walk. Every time he lagged, his captors shoved him forward, sending him, more than once, sprawling onto the ground. Anura lay under the bush and imagined running after his commander. He imagined grabbing one of the guns still littering the floor of the fort and shooting at least one, maybe even two, fighters. He imagined shooting Peiris because he knew what those fighters were planning to do to the Brigadier Commander. But Anura couldn't force himself to move.

He spent the night underneath a hibiscus bush, unable to sleep, curled up beside the whimpering camp dog. When he came out the next morning, he refused to look around him. He refused to see the charred remains covered with ants and flies or acknowledge the rats, mongooses, mice, and crows fighting for bits of rotting flesh. He walked out of the fort, the camp dog limping behind, and followed the road to Batticaloa.

Eventually, Anura found troops also marching toward Batticaloa and he fell in with them. The camp dog followed him the entire way, though it had developed a limp. Anura examined the wounded leg. A tiny piece of shrapnel had been caught in the bed of the dog's paw. Anura removed it with an old piece of metal he found strewn along the road.

At Batticaloa the soldiers told Anura that the generals wanted to talk to him the next morning. They wanted a complete report of what happened at the fort and what happened to Brigadier Commander Peiris. Anura was the only survivor of the attack. Would anyone ever believe that he alone had survived? The Army executed cowards. He snuck away that evening.

—•—◄✦►—•—

Diana and Khan were standing in front of the tank. Diana motioned to Anura. "It's come out." Anura dropped his mop and ran.

The mantis shrimp was dancing again. The only fish left in the tank was the catfish. There were only two snails.

Anura grabbed a green nylon fishnet, stood on tiptoe, and opened the tank. He forced the net into the gravel and scraped as hard as he could. His efforts upended a cloud of dirt and gravel, plants, the catfish's castle. Anura felt arms encircle him and pull him back. "Take it easy," Khan said. "You'll wreck the tank."

Anura stood net in hand, breathing hard. The cloud of dirt and rocks had so muddied the water he could not see a thing. Diana plucked the net from his hand. "You're kind of dangerous with this thing."

The three of them watched the murk. Finally, the mantis shrimp crawled forward out of the dust. It halted just where it had been before. Its buggy eyes spun and focused directly on Anura. Anura's heart lurched. The creature was trying to tell him something. It was trying to tell him it knew everything. It knew about the Tamil girl splayed in the dirt at Elephant Pass, a bullet in her forehead. It saw, as Anura often did in his nightmares, the girl's bike lying beside her, front wheel still spinning. It knew how the soldiers had pointed and laughed and how when they turned their slant eyes to Anura, he had forced a chuckle, to prove he was one of them. It knew the rumors about Brigadier Commander Peiris were true. He was still alive being held in the jungle by the Tigers. The mantis shrimp knew about the camp dog. How it had been waiting for Anura when he left the base at Batticaloa and how it had followed him, limping, most of the way. The mantis shrimp knew how the camp dog's wounded leg slowly developed gangrene until it was too ill to walk. Anura had left the dog in a roadside ditch, still alive, ants filing toward it, crows gathering along side. One crow pecked at the dog's head. The dog tried to bite but couldn't even manage a nip. Anura should have found a rock and killed his companion, to relieve its pain. But he hadn't had the stomach. And the mantis shrimp was telling him it knew the most important thing of all. Anura had never been quite brave enough.

The mantis shrimp waved its claws and charged the glass. It struck hard. The glass tank creaked and moaned. Anura snatched the net from Diana and leapt onto the console. Khan tried to grab Anura, but when the console tottered Khan backed away. A crowd began to surround the tank. Ibrahim came running from the kitchen, crying out to Anura in Sinhala, calling him a mad bugger. The console teetered and protested under Anura's weight but held. He looked down into the tank. Through the cloud of dirt, he saw the mantis shrimp retreat. Anura also saw what the creature hated so much: its own reflection warping in the aquarium glass.

Anura lunged at the mantis shrimp with the net, but the surface of the water deceived him and he missed. The mantis shrimp gathered itself and then lurched forward; its claws hit the side of the tank with a sharp crack. Anura jabbed and missed. He jabbed again and again.

The console groaned; a fissure crept up the side of one leg. A stream of water began to spout from the edges of the aquarium frame. The console teetered momentarily on its crippled leg and then tilted. The aquarium slid forward and crashed onto the mess hall floor. A wave of splintered glass and salt water cascaded toward Khan and Diana. They hopped back just in time.

The console held for one more moment. Then, it too tipped. When it did, Anura spied the mantis shrimp below him, scuttling between shards of broken glass. The mantis shrimp scurried to the edge of the mess hall and ran along the border. It was going to find the one place, hidden far in the Kuwaiti desert, the one small pond of water, where it would thrive. And, as Anura fell, just before his body hit the ground, he understood that he, once again, would have to leave.

War Wounds

$\cdot\cdot\ \equiv\!\!\blacklozenge\!\!\equiv\ \cdot\cdot$

Anoja hoped the phone would not ring that Wednesday evening as it had every Wednesday for the past two years. She would have to lie to her husband again. She hadn't gone to the Australian High Commission as he'd asked. She hadn't made any progress with her immigration application. But the phone did ring at the time when Anoja's sons had gone to bed, when the servant had retired, after Anoja's younger brother, Ranjith, was safely in his bedroom.

"You have the forms? You have filled them out?" her husband demanded.

Always it was the same two questions. This time he hadn't even pretended to be concerned about how she was doing. "I went to a lawyer," Anoja informed him, trying to keep her voice from trembling. "I asked him what would happen to Ranjith-malli."

There was a long pause. She could hear her husband's breathing, soft and distant. "We have already decided. Your brother will take him."

"Aiya says he can't. He says he has no money."

"He's lying. He does a good job. His wife does a job." She explained how her brother had invested with Golden Key, and how he'd lost his savings. She heard the sharp intake of breath. "What a fool."

"He says he already has to do too much," Anoja said. "He has the girls, he's sending money for nenda-amma, and he—"

"All I want to know is when you are coming? When are you bringing my sons, my family?" She watched as a gecko, tinier than normal, skittered across the far wall. It disappeared into a small crack. The room was very hot, and she hadn't turned on the ceiling fan so that the family could save a little money. She took a handkerchief from her nightstand and wiped the beads of sweat from her forehead and the back of her neck.

"I can't leave malli alone here. He's making progress but—"

"It will be for two years only. Then you can sponsor him."

"The lawyer says it's not so easy."

"He's a grown man. Let the government take him. The government did this to malli. Let the government pay the price for his care."

Even though there was no chance that her brother Ranjith could hear her, Anoja dropped her voice. "Malli is all alone here. He has nobody but aiya and me."

"Your aiya does nothing to help. Why should we be saddled with this? Your aiya is settled. He has no ambition. He is happy with the little he has." Her husband was breathing hard now. "But why should he hold us back also? Because we want more than he does? Because we are not so foolish as to invest our life savings with conmen?"

Anoja remained quiet for a beat. "You could come back. Aiya can find you a job. And you have earned so much money—"

"We have planned for this since before we were married." There was nothing in Sri Lanka for Anoja's husband. There were no jobs. If he did find one, he wouldn't make half the money he made in Perth. "I can't live here alone," her husband insisted. "I have already waited too long for you. If you won't come, I can't promise . . ." Her husband's voice trailed off.

Anoja's husband had left for Perth two years ago. She had agreed to stay with the boys, because her husband had not wanted to pull them from school, especially since he was not sure he wanted to stay in Australia. Then six months after her husband left, her brother had arrived. Now, her husband was established in Perth. He worked a secure job as an accountant and had earned a permanent visa. Anoja saw no other possibility than to be with her husband. She had to find a way to leave. It wasn't just that she loved her husband, which she did, deeply. Their lives were interwoven in ways she would never have imagined before marriage. Her house, her money, her sons, everything stemmed from him. When she was young, she had thought it romantic—entirely normal—when people described their spouses and children as limbs of a body. Now she knew how horrible a concept that was. Lose a limb, lose a part of your body, and you ceased to function normally, not just for a short period. Your loss was irrevocable. Anoja had seen that first hand. "I will come," she assured her husband. "I will talk to the doctor tomorrow about government hospitals for malli. I promise." Seconds later she heard the click of the phone as her husband rang off without saying goodbye.

The next morning, as Ranjith descended the stairs, the children started giggling. The hair on one side of Ranjith's head was carefully combed and slicked back. The hair on the other side was tousled and unkempt as if he had just awoken. One side of his face was clean-shaven. A day's growth of beard covered the other. It reminded Anoja of an old book jacket—Dr. Jekyll, Mr. Hyde. The same man split in two halves—one sane, one mad.

This was a common occurrence but every time it happened Anoja's children found it funny. Her eldest, who knew better, snickered the loudest. Anoja understood that the boy laughed not from callousness but out of discomfort. He was the one with the memory of his uncle from before. But because he started to laugh, the other two children felt they could laugh as well. Anoja took one stride toward her eldest son— as soon as he saw her move toward him, he cowered—and raised her hand. She struck him, much harder than she had intended. The heel of her hand connected to his jawbone and sent his head snapping back.

The blow was surprisingly sharp, and the pain, while excruciating, carried with it a frisson of pleasure. Anoja's eldest boy looked up at her and massaged his cheek, wide eyes brimming with tears. Immediately, she knew she had done something very wrong. She wanted to tell him the truth. She wanted to explain. She had hit him because she could not hit her brother. But he was far too young to understand.

Anoja guided Ranjith to the bathroom. She carefully applied a dab of hair gel and combed the right forelock back. She stared at his mirror image. They might have been twins. They shared the same face cut; both had finely chiseled features and large expressive eyes. But Ranjith had a scar running along his right cheek, and a deep indentation on the right side of his head, where the army doctors had removed a piece of his skull to allow his brain to swell. When Anoja combed Ranjith's hair she could feel the raised, nubby surface of yet another scar, three inches long, hidden by his thick black hair. Ranjith accepted her care without protest and without the slightest fidget. Anoja's three boys had ceased being receptive to her caresses sometime around three years old. Yes, when they felt wounded and needy, they'd allow her to wrap her arms around them, demanded it even. But they always decided when and for how long. Ranjith, for all his pain, never stopped her.

She pointed to a note, taped to the bathroom mirror, meant for her younger brother. It reminded him to shave the left side of his face, comb the left side of his hair, and brush the left side of his mouth. "Didn't you remember to read the note, malli?" she prodded.

But he wasn't listening to her. Instead, he was staring at himself in the mirror. "Who is that man?" he demanded. "He looks familiar."

"It s a beautiful man. His name is Ranjith," she said to him. "He is my malli," she told him. "And I love him."

Her brother thought about this for a moment. "I am your malli."

She nodded.

He pointed to himself. "This man is me?"

This exchange occurred less and less frequently. Still, every time it seemed absurd to her, like two children sharing a private riddle, but that wasn't the case. They were adults. The question was sincere, and he needed to hear the answer every time he asked.

Anoja learned the story of what happened to Ranjith not from her brother himself—he had no memory of the event leading up to his injury—but from a former soldier, a friend from Ranjith's regiment. Ranjith was traveling with his regiment near Vidattaltivu when the truck he was riding in hit a Claymore mine. The blast waves and fragments from the explosion had blown out Ranjith's eardrum, fractured his skull, and, according to the doctors, caused a contusion on Ranjith's brain.

When he first came home a year and a half ago, Ranjith could barely hold a conversation. He was angry, liable to lash out at the slightest provocation. He had never hurt anyone around him, but, still, it was frightening to see. He swore and often used sexually suggestive language, and during those times Anoja had to send the boys to their rooms to watch DVDs or play video games. Anoja had had a different servant at that time. Ranjith had accused her of being LTTE. The servant had left the next day, terrified that such an accusation by a former soldier would mean that the police would come question her. Still, Anoja had persisted. She cared for her brother. Everyday she had worked with him. They had used the flashcards with the pictures of common objects and animals—a telephone, a car, a horse. Ranjith had to identify the symbols. At first he'd gotten very few right. Now he was able to identify more than half. Anoja had helped him to keep a notebook of lists: tasks that he needed to complete and steps for the simplest things like answering a telephone or combing his hair. Anoja had even felt comfortable enough to hire recently another servant with the extra money her husband sent.

Ranjith's soldier friend had visited every week for three months. Anoja had loved those visits because the soldier was only a boy—early twenties at most—and was charming and sweet and very talkative. He spoke of adventures and battles and described Ranjith as brave and sociable and well liked by his comrades. It gave Anoja solace to know that Ranjith's life in the army had not been miserable.

Then the soldier stopped coming. He did not call or send a letter. Ranjith—and Anoja—never received an explanation for the absence. Anoja had assumed the friend had grown weary of memories of war. He had met a woman and gotten married and had begun a normal life. Even though she was sorry she would not see him again, Anoja did not blame the soldier for wanting to move on.

It was a nurse at the hospital where she took Ranjith for his tests who told Anoja the truth. Ranjith's friend had committed suicide. The news had shocked Anoja: a man who had survived unscathed—no visible war wounds, no scars—who was whole and beautiful had, after all he'd seen and survived, killed himself in his own home. The soldier had returned. He was safe. How could he not have known that? Anoja wondered if Ranjith ever thought about suicide. Perhaps he no longer had a concept of such a thing.

Anoja sat in the hospital waiting room that morning as they tested Ranjith to monitor his progress. She had found the cleanest looking seat in a line of broken and filthy-looking bucket chairs. In the far corner, a television set broadcast a cricket match. Anoja didn't like cricket—though Ranjith had been before the war mad for the sport— but it wouldn't have mattered if she had. The screen flickered every few seconds so that it was painful to focus on for too long. The woman next to Anoja had a bandage over one eye and a bandage covering her forearm. The gauze was stained and caked with dried blood and pus, and the woman exuded the scent of onions. Did the smell emanate from the wound itself or had this woman been cooking earlier that morning? Both possibilities made Anoja feel queasy. Anoja folded in on herself to keep from brushing against the woman.

She had had a pleasant conversation with Ranjith in the tuk-tuk on the way to the hospital. They'd talked about her sons, and she'd shared some gossip about the neighbor. Ranjith had been able to follow what she was telling him, and he'd given logical, reasonable responses. When he couldn't think of a word, he remained calm and gave a good description of what he was trying to say instead of losing his temper and punching his forehead as in the past.

Ranjith's doctor came out of the examination room and gestured for Anoja to follow him. They stood in a recess at the end of the hospital corridor. A nurse wheeled a patient past: a man whose skin was flaking in raw patches from head to toe. Anoja shivered and glanced away.

"Your brother is making remarkable progress," the doctor assured her. "You deserve a lot of credit for your patience and diligence."

She took a deep breath and blurted. "My husband is in Perth. He wants me to come."

"That's a good thing," the doctor replied. "There are good neurologists in—"

"No, you don't understand. I won't be able to take him with me. I want to leave him in a special hospital." Two mornings before, the immigration lawyer had explained to her, as she sipped the cup of tea he had given her, that Australia was unlikely to grant a visa to Ranjith, because Anoja was not the only living relative and because Ranjith was so sick.

A fly, so engorged with blood it could barely stay aloft, buzzed at the doctor's face. He swatted at it distractedly. "Isn't there anyone else who can take him? A sibling? Maybe a cousin?"

"I have an older brother, but he doesn't have room in his house."

"These episodes are much rarer. If your husband can only wait a little. A year perhaps. I'm very heartened by what I'm seeing." There was a long pause. "Has Ranjith done anything in any way that has seemed out of sorts, unduly hostile?"

Anoja shook her head. During the first months of his recovery, one of the nurses had claimed Ranjith had been sexually aggressive with her. There was no proof, and the nurse was later sacked for other lies. But the doctors had been concerned nonetheless.

Anoja took a deep breath. "Sir, will he ever be able to hold a job?"

The doctor smiled kindly. "Ranjith has his pension. He won't have to work unless he wants to."

"The lawyer says it will be easier for malli to immigrate to Australia if he can do a job."

The doctor tucked his chin against his neck and stared at the floor.

His voice was patient and kind, but there was an unmistakable tired-ness, as if he encountered these types of questions everyday. "The truth is these things are unknowable. I have seen patients make extraordi-nary progress after horrible injuries. There is always the possibility."

"Is there a hospital for him?" Anoja repeated.

The doctor took a long time to answer. When he spoke, he chose his words carefully. "A mental hospital would be a risk for a patient like Ranjith. He's making progress precisely because you are so diligent in caring from him. Being part of society, the normal flow of it, is very important for someone suffering what he is suffering from. Do you understand?" Anoja nodded. "If you give him some time, I feel sure that he will make a full recovery. He may be able to live alone then. But a mental hospital is a place of last resort. It is a place the sickest people go. If Ranjith was violent with you, if he was liable to hurt himself then I would say hospitalize him. But know that such a place will hurt him more than help." Anoja nodded again. She knew what the doctor was saying was right. The night before, because she was curious, she had looked up Sri Lankan mental hospitals on her son's computer. She had found a web site of photographs by a Britisher who had spent some time documenting a nearby hospital. She had forced herself to click on each photograph—there were at least a hundred. It would be one thing if she could come and check on him, make sure the hospital was caring for her brother, but once she'd left who knew when she would be able to return. If Ranjith's friend had been so willing to take his own life while at home, with his friends and family, what would happen to Ranjith left alone in a place like a mental hospital, among so many sick, sad people?

Anoja thanked the doctor for his time.

⋯⋯

That evening, she sat with her boys while they spoke with their father on Skype. Her husband looked happy, if a little tired, and he had lost at least a stone. She always felt a tightness in her chest when she saw him like that. He lived with three other men, Sri Lankan immigrants as well. None of them, he had told Anoja, could cook well.

Anoja was about to tell her boys to get ready for bed. She wanted a chance to talk to her husband alone. She would tell him the truth. She would tell him that she couldn't send Ranjith to a hospital but there was good news. She had read that the government was building a home for soldiers like Ranjith, soldiers who had suffered serious injuries in the war. It would have only fifty beds but the government was promising to build others around the country. She would go back to aiya. Maybe she could use this information to talk aiya into allowing Ranjith to stay with his family for a few months.

She heard something break in the kitchen, followed by Ranjith swearing. She got up to see what happened. When she neared the kitchen, she saw Ranjith first. He was standing with his back toward the doorway. She saw the servant woman, standing with her back towards him. Ranjith was very close to her, saying something to her. The fragments of a broken saucer lay at the servant's feet. Startled, Anoja took a step backward. The boys had left some of their schoolbooks on the dining table. She'd been too surprised by what she'd seen to accost her brother directly. Instead, she picked up her son's schoolbook and dropped it on the floor. Anoja stepped again into the doorway of the kitchen.

The servant woman was gone. Ranjith was crouched and trying to pick up the shards. When he saw Anoja, he looked up. "Stupid, she broke the . . ." He stared at the floor, struggling. "She broke all the pieces."

"What were you saying to her?" Anoja demanded.

"All the pieces," Ranjith muttered. "The pieces to that . . ."

Anoja stepped over the broken saucer and grabbed the dustpan and the brush. She swept the remains of the saucer as her brother watched. After she had emptied the dustpan into the rubbish bin, she turned to Ranjith. He was still crouched staring at the floor. "Malli, you can't hurt people," she said. "You can't scare them." Ranjith didn't reply.

Anoja made her way to the servant's room in the back of the house. The light was off. She put her ear to the door. There was no noise. She considered knocking, but what would she say. She didn't know what had happened, and she was already beginning to think that perhaps she overreacted. The girl hadn't yelled or spoken out. Surely, if she was being hurt she would have screamed for help, out of fear. Anoja was far too easily willing to think the worst of Ranjith. She always had been.

When Anoja was fourteen and Ranjith was eight thugs had robbed their house while the family was inside. One of them, a young boy, no more than nineteen, had kept guard over Anoja, Ranjith, and their parents in one of the bedrooms while the rest ransacked the house. (Their eldest brother, their aiya, was already married and had moved away.) The hora had sweated and paced the room and looked more nervous than threatening. Perhaps to calm himself, he had started chatting with Ranjith. He noticed the toy—a mutant ninja turtle action figure—that Ranjith clutched to his chest. The two joked about Dragonball and Mutant Ninja Turtles, movies, and superheroes. The guard, who reeked of urine as if he'd wet his pants while breaking into the house, sounded so very, very young. When his friends had finished taking all the knives, everything that was made of metal, anything of value, all Anoja's mother's family jewelry, after they tore open all the cushions on the settee and destroyed all the furniture in the sitting room, after they slit the throat of Anoja's pet dog who could not have possibly done them any harm, the thug's friends came back to get him. As the guard turned to leave, Ranjith had given him his Donatello action figure as a gift.

The family had mocked Ranjith. Anoja's father called him too sweet and accused him of being feminine. The mother wouldn't talk to Ranjith for days after. Anoja tormented him the most. She blamed him for the death of her dog. She accused him of being its killer. She accused Ranjith of helping the thugs—maybe he'd been the one who let them in. He'd left the gate open. She had despised him for being so weak, for being stupid enough to like a man who was harming them. She had told the story to every one who would listen, visitors and relatives. She brought her friends home, and they mocked him also. Her torment continued for months after her parents relented and started treating Ranjith kindly again.

Anoja wondered now if that was why Ranjith had joined the Sri Lanka Army. Ranjith had wanted to prove he could fight. He wanted to prove how strong he could be. She wondered if it was her family that had made him like this. Not the war. Not the Sri Lanka Army. Not the LTTE. Not the Claymore mine. Her family had taken a boy who was sweet and gentle, who thought about others, and made him into a person who swore at people, who could not control himself, his body or his temper. She was the one who had brought this man about.

When Anoja returned to the room, only the eldest remained at the computer. He was playing a game of solitaire. Anoja asked him if his father had left any messages for her. He shook his head distractedly and didn't look up from the screen. No message, nothing, she prodded. The son screwed up his face. He didn't say anything about you. She ran her hand through his hair. When he still didn't look at her, she gripped one side of his head and planted a kiss on the side of the boy's forehead. He squirmed but when she released him she saw a flicker of a smile. She told her son to get ready for bed and closed the door behind her.

The next morning, she found breakfast ready for them. When she called the servant woman to come help her with the boys, the servant claimed, in a frail, tweedy voice, to be feeling sick. She couldn't get out of bed. Anoja hadn't had the time to question the servant, and when the woman didn't come out of her room to help with lunch, Anoja quashed the uneasiness she felt and let the servant be. The servant should sleep off whatever was bothering her.

Late that afternoon, Anoja took Ranjith to visit their elder brother. Her aiya had called earlier that day. He said he wanted to speak to Anoja in person. She imagined he was only going to reiterate that he couldn't help her, and she prepared to beg.

They sat together, her aiya and her, in his dining room. Ranjith sat in the back garden. She could just see him through the doorway. He was looking out, stroking aiya's Alsatian.

Anoja's aiya was ten years older than her. He had already left the house and married while she was still young. He worked as a driver for a travel agency that catered to rich foreigners and wealthy expats who had come for vacation. His wife was a secretary at one of the large banks. They had four girls—one nineteen, one twelve, one seven, one toddler.

There was a console to the side. On it sat their parents' wedding photograph. Her thaththa had died eight years ago; her amma shortly after. There was an aunt in Kandy. She lived alone, but she was old and would not have the strength to care for Ranjith. Maybe later, when Ranjith was better. Maybe he could go and live with her. They could use the money his pension provided, and he could maybe even be a help to her.

Anoja's aiya wouldn't look at her. Anoja leaned forward and stretched her hands across the dining room table toward him. "Please, I must go," she begged. "He is so alone in Australia and it isn't right for him to be apart from us." Her brother didn't respond. "The government is promising to build a home in Anuradhapura, a guest house for injured soldiers."

The brother scoffed. "The government is always making promises."

Anoja glanced in Ranjith's direction. He was still sitting with his hand on the dog's head. A murti of Ganesh had been mounted over the threshold to the kitchen. She could almost laugh at that. It seemed fitting somehow that Ganesh would hang over Ranjith's head. "I can't be expected to care for him for the rest of my life," she said.

Her brother nodded his head slowly. "You're right, nangi. This is why I asked you to come to talk with me. We should help you. It isn't right that you take the burden for caring for malli." She blinked and waited to make sure that he had really spoken those words. She hadn't just imagined them. Her aiya reached over and put his hand on her arm. "We want to help you. It's only right." She nodded and whispered a hoarse thank you

"We'll have to hire someone to work with him. You will have to send money to help us." She nodded vigorously. "And after two years, you will sponsor him to go to Australia."

She started. She hadn't mentioned anything about her visit with the lawyer. "Of course, we will do that," she lied.

"He will be better off there in Australia," her brother said. "They must have good doctors. Better than here." She thought momentarily of telling him what the immigration lawyer had told her, but she couldn't bring herself to. In two years, Ranjith would be better and there would be new alternatives for them. The doctor had said as much.

"We will do this. If you take him now, when we can, we will bring him to Australia."

The brother studied his hands for a moment. "How does malli give you money?"

Anoja bit her lower lip. "I don't know what you mean?"

"The money for his food and for his clothes? You take this directly from his pension."

"He isn't simple," Anoja mumbled. "Malli keeps a notebook. He can do his sums." She knew what her brother wanted to hear. "I cash his check for him," she admitted. "Then he gives me what I need. But I also give a lot to him."

"We can't be expected to spend on him," her brother said. "I already have so many things I must spend on." He started ticking them off.

"That money. He saves it," Anoja interrupted. "In case he ends up alone with no one to look after him." She hesitated. Anoja didn't want to protest too much. She didn't want her aiya to change his mind.

Her brother sighed. He stood up from the table. She looked up at him beseechingly. "This is a good thing. You will earn merit for the next life."

Her brother snorted. "It is this life I am most worried about." He told Anoja he was going to get his wife so they could begin to make arrangements.

After her brother left the room, Anoja's twelve-year-old niece sidled up to her chair. "Punchi-amma, can you help me? Thaththa said you were good at maths."

Anoja put her arm around her niece's waist and pulled the girl to her. The niece placed her workbook on the table. She pointed to a problem.

Anoja started to explain to the girl how to calculate the answer on her own. The girl was leaning over the book, so that Anoja could not see her face. All that was visible was the top of her head, the neat sliver of grayish-pink skin revealed by the part. The girl was lean and long-limbed, but Anoja could also feel, as she held her, that the girl's hips were starting to become full.

Anoja thought of the night before, of the servant. What had she seen? Anoja's niece gave the right answer to the question. Anoja nodded and forced a smile.

Ranjith had pinned the servant to the kitchen counter with his body, one arm blocking her so she couldn't leave. His other hand covered the servant's mouth. Anoja felt a warmth creep up her neck and face. Why had she not understood earlier?

The niece wrote down the answer to the next problem. When Anoja told her she was right, the girl glanced up from her workbook and grinned. It was easy to explain what Anoja saw the night before. The servant had upset Ranjith somehow. She had done something to startle him. Ranjith was never aggressive with the boys or with Anoja, and Ranjith would never mistreat his own niece. Or Anoja was misremembering. Her anxiety, the nearness of getting what she wanted, caused her mind to exaggerate. She was being hysterical, imagining things that weren't. Yet every time she assured herself, Anoja felt a churning in her stomach. What would she tell herself if something happened? What excuse would she give then?

The niece pointed to another problem in her workbook and Anoja demonstrated the solution. Anoja considered confessing to her aiya what she thought she had seen the night before. She would let him provide the correct interpretation. At least then, if her brother reneged, Anoja could claim truthfully that he was the one who had made the decision. It would not be her responsibility. But Anoja also knew, in that same moment, with certainty, that she could no longer be sure if her aiya would make the right choice, for the right reasons. He hadn't yet.

The girl recited a line of numbers, her voice sweet and lilting, completely oblivious to Anoja's anguish. Anoja experienced a flash of anger, bitter tasting and blinding, at the girl. She wanted to shove her niece away, to snap at her that she was a stupid little thing for not knowing the answers already. If the girl had not come to her at that moment, Anoja would have left the house ready to go to Australia. At the very least, Anoja deserved to see the girl blink back tears.

But Anoja bit down hard on the inside of her cheek and allowed the anger to ebb. There was no point in such a show. It would not provide what Anoja most needed, neither hope nor relief. It seemed the best course, the only course, was to keep the cruelty contained within her, even if no one ever saw or gave her credit for what she was doing, even if it did Anoja herself no good.

She squeezed her niece tight and praised her. The girl giggled and writhed. She grabbed her workbook and ran from the room. Anoja's aiya returned; his wife followed close behind. He started to pull a chair from the table. Anoja stood. "I should take Ranjith and go home," she said. "It's late, and the boys will be back from school."

"But there's more to discuss."

"I do not think this will work, aiya." Anoja's voice quavered. "You have the little one. You are both working. You don't have the time to care for anyone else."

"We said we'll hire someone. You will send us some money—"

Anoja put up a hand. "You have to monitor this person. Do you have the time? Ranjith is doing well with me. He'll heal faster if I continue working with him."

Her aiya's brow furrowed. For a moment, he seemed genuinely concerned. "What about Australia?"

She could barely look at her brother; the desire to change her mind was so strong. "I will have to stay here a little longer." She stared at the ground until it became a soft blur. "What to do?"

She didn't wait for him to say anything else; she didn't wait for her own mind to change out of weakness. She strode through the kitchen into the garden. She found Ranjith staring off and put a hand on his shoulder. All those years ago, all those horrible things she'd done to him, and he'd never told on her, never complained to their parents.

He had always lied when they noticed a welt or a bruise. He had kept this secret not because she threatened him not to tell—she had secretly wanted him to—but out of loyalty—and love. "What are you looking at, malli?" she prodded gently.

Ranjith closed his eyes for a moment and pursed his lips in concentration. The doctors had told Anoja that many of Ranjith's childhood memories had been erased by the injury, but that he would regain most of them eventually. "The sky," her brother finally managed. "I was looking at the sky."

⸺ ✦ ⸺

When Anoja returned home, she found her sons alone seated in front of the television. She demanded to know where the servant was. They shrugged. They told her that they had not seen her since they'd returned from school.

Anoja walked into the kitchen. No sign of the woman. She walked to the back of the house, to the servant's room. The door was ajar. She pushed it open to reveal a room that had been emptied of everything but the cot and a SriLankan Air calendar still tacked onto the wall.

She returned to the kitchen. Ranjith was seated with the boys watching television. She pulled tins from the cupboards; she would have to make the evening's dinner on her own. She started to imagine the story she would tell her husband that evening if he called. She would send him the children—her sons. This would be her promise to him. He would know that she would never leave them for long—she would rather die than abandon them—and then he would also know that she was doing what she could. He would accept that. She would promise him that she would work hard to make Ranjith better. She would work hard to find him another home, a good one where he would be safe. Once this was achieved, then she would come.

Unicorn

—◆ ≡◆≡ ◆—

"We had an old master then, you are the new master now," the Tamil servant said as he handed a teacup to one of the guests. The Major, one of the hosts, smiled benevolently but Lieutenant Colonel Lalith Weerakoon cringed. The servant must have thought he was helping the officers impress the group of women seated across from them, but it was a poor choice of words and faintly improper. The women did not so much as glance at the servant; they smiled only at the Major. All but one of them seemed quite taken with the handsome and young officer, and they didn't appear to register what the servant had just said. Lalith told the servant to leave the teacups next to the samovar and step away. He wanted to spare the man the need to display more subservience and the women the embarrassment of having this man prostrate himself before them. As the Major beckoned to the group to pour themselves tea, Lalith sidled next to the servant and reminded him quietly there were no more masters—not Tamil Tiger, not Sri Lanka Army. The servant bowed to Lalith and repeated, "Thank you, Lieutenant Colonel. Thank you." When Lalith turned back to his guests, he noticed one of the women—the one who, so far, during their tea, had refused to talk—watching with a look somewhere between pity and consternation as the servant waddled into the kitchen. He nodded at her, but she pretended as if she had not noticed.

Lalith was an engineer serving the Sri Lanka Electrical and Mechanical Engineers, Sixth Battalion, Unicorn Division, part of the demining operation in Mullaitivu. He had served in the Sri Lanka Army for the entire duration of the civil war, nearly thirty years. The women sitting in front of him were bankers from Colombo—presidents and vice-presidents within their divisions. The area had once been under the control of the Tigers but was now overseen by the Sri Lankan military and dangerous despite the fact that the war was over. Yellow ticker tape still marked wide swaths of land pocked by mines. But the military wanted to involve civilian organizations in reconstruction as soon as possible. They had missed such an opportunity in the Nineties with disastrous consequences for the entire country. These women bankers, then, were especially important being, as they were, so close to the one resource any reconstruction needed most—money. The guests were to be given a tour that morning of the former Tiger leader's bunker, a former Tiger training ground, and the Tiger-run city. That was why Lalith and the Major were in military uniform sipping tea with their guests in the sitting room of a house, long ago abandoned by its owners.

Lalith knew one of the women through his wife, who lived in Colombo. He knew the woman's name but referred to her in his mind as 'the cat' because she had balal æs, green eyes, and because she never quite looked at anyone directly but always cut her gaze slyly. The other women were attractive in their own ways. All well-dressed and manicured, sporting jewelry they'd bought, no doubt, from some jeweler in Liberty Plaza in Colombo, and they looked to be nearing their mid-forties—twenty years older than the Major they were flirting with and much closer to Lalith in age. Well, four of them were flirting—or more accurately jostling—for the Major's attention. One sat silently with her knees together, back ramrod straight, staring into her teacup as if she were trying to decode within it some secret message. She was also dressed differently than the others; her blouse and slacks looked to be a cut not typical to Colombo high society, and she wore a too-ornate necklace, a circle of crimson gemstones that appeared in a certain light like congealed droplets of blood. Maybe she was not just dumb but deaf as well, because she didn't seem to be trying to follow the conversation. A breeze wafted through the room carrying with it the scent of the bougainvillea bushes bordering HQ. He leaned forward to address her. He spoke in English so that she would know he too was educated, sophisticated, and this would put her at ease. "You are excited about seeing the Tiger bunker?" The mute looked up from her teacup, eyes wide. She was able to hear as well.

But before the mute could respond, the cat leaned toward him and purred, "I saw your wife." Lalith realized that he hadn't thought of his wife that day, or even yesterday for that matter, and the sudden image the cat's statement conjured chastened him. He looked over at the mute. She had slid back in her chair and returned to examining her teacup. It occurred to him the cat had spoken not out of any real desire to engage Lalith in a conversation but to protect the mute. She did this not the way that men did—out of camaraderie and shared mission—but out of that silent pact made between women to protect the weakest among them. Lalith wondered then if something terrible had happened to the mute— it was certainly possible the way things had changed in Sri Lanka.

The cat dipped at the waist, and, when she did, her blouse opened a little to reveal the swell of her breasts, squashed together and served up in black lace cups. But the glimpse didn't arouse as much as remind Lalith that he hadn't seen—or touched—a woman's breasts in over a year. He struggled to ward of an immediate, irrepressible sorrow. "How is my wife?" Lalith asked, though he regretted the question as soon as it was uttered.

"Don't you know?" the cat smirked. He nodded. She was playing pucks with him.

Lalith stood up. Though he was in mid-sentence, the Major hopped up at the same time as Lalith and gestured at the door. The women left their teacups on the table and Lalith ushered them down the stairs before the servant could come out and offer another awkward, potentially embarrassing observation.

As they strolled together to the van that would carry the women on their tour, the Major pointed to an armored personal carrier positioned on its own in a bed of dirt as one might a garden statue. "This is a Unicorn," he announced, his tone a combination of ostentation and reverence.

The APC was painted camouflage, boxy, all armor plating, metal hull and bullet-proof glass. Its snub-nosed cowl and the way the body of the vehicle appeared to hunch on its chassis resembled not an animal so elegant as a unicorn but a bulldog. The Major gazed at it with the awe boys reserved for their favorite toys, He turned toward Lalith. "The Lieutenant Colonel designed it." It wasn't true. Lalith was only one of many individuals responsible for the Unicorn's final design.

The woman nodded their heads solemnly and with approval. Lalith looked over at the mute. She was circling the APC. The mute neared Lalith as she completed her circle. He felt the sudden, odd urge for her to notice him. "Without these Unicorns so many more soldiers and civilians would have died," he said. "We've saved many, many lives." But the women were already turning away. They weren't interested in numbers. They were only interested in reaffirming they were bankrolling the side that had won. This Unicorn turned garden ornament was all the proof they needed. The mute was the only one who had listened, but she returned his gaze with a tight-lipped stare. He had to force himself not to stare back at her.

The Major gestured to the van. The women's obvious giddiness at the prospect of the tour made Lalith happy as well. These women would be awed by what the army had conquered, as they were by the Unicorn APC. The army had fought for the well-being of women like this, and their approval not only meant money but some sense that all those cosseted in Colombo recognized the sacrifice made for them. The women would understand and be proud, and, maybe, hopefully, by the end of the day Lalith would manage to get the mute to answer at least one of the questions he put to her.

For decorum's sake, Lalith and the Major rode in a jeep that trailed their guest's van. To reach the Tiger bunker, they had to turn off the main highway onto a dirt road. The road was heavily pockmarked: potholes and deep tracks left by the APCs. Lalith's driver knew how to navigate the road, but the women's Colombo driver seemed befuddled. Every time he veered to avoid a pothole, he managed to send the van plummeting into some crevice. The van moved slowly but raised a considerable amount of dust and pebbles as it did. The pebbles thwacked against the side of the van and must have sounded to the van's occupants like an artillery barrage. Lalith's driver managed to stay far enough behind that they could avoid much of the dust and the rocks, but the stench of petrol exhaust overwhelmed Lalith, one of the two main odors Lalith had come to equate with army life—the other of men in close quarters. He thought of the women in the van and the scent of perfume they exuded. His own countrymen separated by a little over two hundred miles had led such different lives than him.

That observation reminded him he was proud of who he was: an officer in the Sri Lanka Army. He had written as much in an opinion piece published in *The Island* commemorating the army victory. Lalith was especially fond of one line: *Politicians establish culture, government, nomocracy, but it is soldiers like us, whose ingenuity built the fortifications high enough, and dangerous enough, to keep the barbarians, from the Gauls to the Tigers, in the wilderness where they belong.* The newspaper had given his letter a prominent position on their editorial page. He'd received congratulations from his friends and then it had been forgotten, though he wondered now if he could find some way to mention the letter to the mute, perhaps even show her a clipping.

Lalith and the Major chatted amiably as they drove, though the Major had very little to say about the women. Finally, Lalith asked the Major directly about the mute. Had she said anything at all to him? The Major appeared puzzled. Because Lalith could not remember the woman's name—come to think of it, had she or her friends ever told Lalith her name?—and only referred to her as the mute, the Major didn't know to whom Lalith was referring. Before Lalith could explain their jeep hit a pothole. He hovered, suspended momentarily mid-air. He landed on the seat hard enough to knock the air out of him. By the time he regained his composure, the Major had moved on to the logistics of building shower pumps and latrines in Mannar, and Lalith decided that pressing the matter would appear odd. Instead, he suggested that the Major lead the tour. This would give Lalith the chance to watch the women, maybe even talk with the mute. The Major appeared surprised but also pleased.

As they began to move deeper and deeper into the jungle, the road grew darker and the van and the jeep slowed to a near crawl. Tiny slivers of light pierced the dense canopy, bright winking stars in the murky darkness. Lalith wondered about the women inside. Were they frightened or excited? He thought of the mute. He had decided she hadn't suffered some trauma at the hands of men. She didn't seem afraid of Lalith or the Major. There was in fact something oddly bold about her silence, a disapproval. She was one of those that believed what the Western journalists wrote about the shelling of thousands of civilians.

The Major beckoned to the group to follow him. Lalith and the Major trailed behind. The first room they entered was a bedroom. A four-post bed stood in one corner. The mattress had been stripped bare and the fabric was stained with sweat and age. Over the bed hung a framed portrait of the Tiger leader in camouflage standing next to a red flag, an actual tiger leaping from a ring of bullets. On a far wall rested a garment rack; a neatly pressed and folded combat uniform hung from one of the rungs. The air tasted heavy on the tongue and faintly bitter. The room had been reconstituted to resemble one of those "this-is-how-they-lived" displays found in museums with only the velvet rope barrier missing. But there was a sparse—haphazard— feel to the whole creation that put Lalith off a bit as if a child had pieced this all together. It reminded him not of a terrorist hideout but of some twisted version of a tot's dollhouse.

The Major rattled on about this being the place where the evil terrorist mastermind had plotted the deaths of so many innocents. The women listened raptly, nodding their heads the way children do to a bedtime story they had heard many times before. Lalith ignored the Major and studied the room. He hated this place. The room. The bunker. It wasn't that this was the seat of luxury that bothered Lalith. That was a piece of propaganda that the military always perpetuated about vanquished leaders: from Hitler to Saddam Hussein. Men whose lives were built around the principles of discipline and self-abnegation loved to level at the enemy a lasciviousness—as if enjoying life might be a crime. No, what struck Lalith was how spare the bunker really was. The Tigers had bred their evil on very little.

Just then, as if she had read his mind, the mute looked over at him. She wasn't listening to the Major. She was taking in the room. Had she come to the same conclusion as Lalith had? He edged closer to her and started to speak. Just then the Major addressed Lalith with some question about the bunker: its size and the type of materials used. Lalith answered quickly and turned his attention back to the mute, but the mute was no longer standing next to him. Instead, the cat had taken her place. "You can feel that man's evil," the cat meowed "It's as if he's sitting right in front of me." She balled her right hand into a fist and extended the index finger toward the bed. She jerked her finger quickly up, mimicking the recoil of a gun. Lalith blinked and the cat gave him a heavy-lidded, knowing smile.

He tapped the cat on the arm. "I want to ask you about her," Lalith said, nodding in the direction of the mute.

"Who?" the cat replied, lightly.

The Major motioned to a darkened doorway. He was going to show them the next level of the bunker. The cat bounced after him without waiting for Lalith's reply.

The doorway led to a wooden stairway so narrow as to allow for the passage of one person at a time. The Major entered first, followed by the women. Lalith brought up the rear, a position he'd maneuvered for himself because it placed him behind the mute. He planned to ask her a question directly, on the staircase, where she could not easily elude him.

The first level stood above ground, but the remaining floors reached nearly fifteen meters deep. The steps were makeshift at best, wood thrown together to create enough of a semblance of a staircase for sol-diers to get up and down. It didn't help that the staircase creaked and with each step exuded a fungal stench. The electrical system for the bunker had been destroyed so the stairway was lit now by a few light bulbs strung along the perimeter, powered by a mobile generator. There were long passageways of near darkness and while Lalith had traversed enough of these underground bunkers to feel sure-footed, the women moved slowly, hands outstretched so that they could use the concrete wall as a guide. The mute was focused only on making her way down step-by-step, and, if he spoke to her, he might distract her enough that she tripped or otherwise hurt herself.

Halfway down, a rush of cool, dank air hit Lalith; the transition from the swollen, roiling heat of the surface to chill reminded Lalith, every time, that Dante had chosen to freeze the innermost, final cir-cle of hell. They passed close enough to a light bulb that Lalith could make out the mute's face. He realized with some amusement she was mouthing oaths against the stairs, against her friends, against her folly in finding herself in this predicament. He experienced a surge of fond-ness for her.

Just then, the generator sputtered and the lights flickered. The mute teetered, her arms flailing wildly for something to help her bal-ance. Lalith reached forward to grab her elbow but somehow missed so that he was left clutching at nothing. He nearly lost his own balance in that moment and managed to keep himself from falling only by bracing his shoulder against the cement wall. When he looked over at the mute, she had regained her balance and was now navigating the remaining steps quickly and agilely. Not only that but the Major and the other women had already reached the bottom. The Major stared up at Lalith with a confused, concerned expression.

The Major had started his speech by the time Lalith had made his way to the bottom. He was giving an overview of the basic structure, the density of the concrete walls, the function of each of the levels, the fact that there was a secret passageway that would have acted as an escape route. The Major's voice reverberated in the concrete and steel enclosure, each word punctuated by the dripping of moisture from what remained of the bunker's interior plumbing. The cement walls secreted an intestinal ooze that glistened in the faint light of the lone bulb that hung from the ceiling. Parts of the wall and floor were badly stained, a type of bacterial corrosion that had spread rapidly in the past few weeks. The light wasn't strong enough to illuminate the ceiling above and the darkness arced over the group like a protective dome. The air stank of mildew and faintly of burnt charcoal and sulfur, a rotten egg smell that was all the more unsettling for being faint. The darkness, the rotten breath and the constant 'drip, drip' reminded Lalith of special effects, and Lalith couldn't help but feel that whole thing was a bit over-contrived. Worse, this business of preserving the Tiger's bunker carried with it a faint whiff of nostalgia perverted, as if the soldiers didn't want the war to end.

One of the women coughed gently, then raised her hand. Everyone turned to look at her. "What exactly are we supposed to be seeing?"

On cue, the generator gave a spasmodic, guttural cough and then quit. All the bulbs dimmed and they were left standing in the dark. The women gasped. The Major swore. Seconds later, the beam of a flashlight loomed over the heads of the women and began swinging towards the generator. Lalith thought of going to help, but as he moved toward the second light, he heard the Major give the generator a quick, sharp kick and that was enough to get it going again. The lights flickered back on. Lalith ushered the women back up the stairs.

Lalith found himself having to help one of the women by holding her elbow and taking each step very slowly. By the time they reached the top the Major and two of the women had moved to one corner of the bunker. In the other corner, in front of a bedside table, stood the mute and the cat. They were staring at a squat metal object the size of a rice cooker. The cat asked what it was. "It's a centrifuge. For testing blood," Lalith replied, "for plasma separation, specifically." He caught the mute's eye. "He," Lalith nodded at the portrait hanging on the wall, "was a diabetic. His men used this to test his insulin." The cat and the mute watched him. Their gaze felt disconcerting and he found himself struggling to explain. "This proves the lengths he went to hide himself," Lalith added. "He was a hard man to defeat. So many people died because of him."

The cat and the mute turned their gaze from Lalith and studied the centrifuge. "So you kept a pot with *his* blood?" the cat mused.

Lalith furrowed his brow. "Of course not. It was cleaned a long time ago."

The cat prodded it with her finger. "Maybe if I rub it a Tiger *jinn* will pop out."

The Major rapped the cat's wrist, and she jerked her finger back. "Don't touch things," he admonished. "You'll disturb it all." But he didn't like the sound of his words once he said them. He sounded like a schoolmarm.

The Major signaled to Lalith that he wanted to speak to him. As Lalith turned to hear the Major out, he caught sight of the mute still staring at the centrifuge, her face scrunched in an expression of repulsion. The cat had joined the other women and none of them looked in her direction. Lalith had never actually seen anyone address the mute. None of her friends had spoken to her. Not one of them had touched her, and she hadn't actually addressed anyone. An ominous thought came to Lalith. She wasn't real. He was seeing things.

Lalith dismissed the idea as quickly as it occurred to him. Of course, this was all nonsense. It was the kind of thought that came unbidden like a temptation to weakness, the habit of an untrained mind. The Major was speaking to him now, and Lalith tried to focus on the Major's words. He recognized he needed to stop thinking about the mute. He had, for god's sake, tried to touch her on the stairs. He could see *The Island* headline now: "Woman Molested by Lieutenant Colonel While on War Tour." That's all the security forces needed right now. And what would his defense be? *I thought she might be a raksha.* He shivered. It was this place, he thought, the bunker. Why had they chosen to preserve it? The madman was dead, they had vanquished him, and yet he still had a way of bespoiling their intentions, of allowing his madness to seep through their every action.

42

The military—armies, soldiers, battles, strategies—had fascinated Lalith even as a very young boy. He read avidly the exploits of all the great military leaders regardless of which side they were on. Years before, a batchmate of his, now living in the States, had mailed a copy of a famous general's autobiography to him. Lalith mulled one passage for days, had written it in his journal, had repeated it to himself as if it were poetry: *and having thus only the choice of evils—war now so terrible and successful that none can dream of rebellion hereafter, or everlasting war with all these evils magnified a hundred fold hereafter— we have no other course to take.* Overwhelming brutality or the everlasting war. That had been the choice for the Security Forces in Sri Lanka as well. And that was the role of men like this famous general, even Lalith himself, to take on themselves the hard, moral choices.

Or that's what Lalith had told himself until recently. Everywhere an army went it tread on what had been or would soon be broken. The military's feats were meant to be utilitarian, to last—like all Lalith's fortifications—only long enough to ensure the battle was won and the enemy kept at bay. This army's choice to linger in a place they helped destroy, seemed to Lalith, neither hard nor moral but about the army needing purpose, any purpose. But who was to blame for that? What *did* you do with an entire army once the war finished?

That evening, after they had finished the tour, Lalith escorted the women back to the Security Forces HQ for an early dinner. The Major had taken three of the women to find some place they could wash before the meal. Lalith sat with the cat and the mute on the verandah sharing between them a plate of short eats—fish cutlets and meat patties. The cat sipped at a ginger tea. The mute sat next to her. The cat had spoken animatedly about what she saw and asked additional

43

questions. The mute still hadn't said a word. Finally, Lalith couldn't restrain himself. He turned to her and blurted, "Well, my Philomela, you have had nothing to say the whole time?" The mute narrowed her eyes at him and a tremor passed over her face. He had meant the sobriquet as a gentle ribbing, but she appeared offended. He experienced a dull thudding in his stomach.

The cat tut-tutted. "That's not a nice thing to say," she chided. "Anyway, my friend has a tongue, and she can be quite devilish in the way she uses it." The mute turned to the cat and raised her eyebrows. Lalith's eyes widened. He knew the cat had a sense of humor, but even she didn't usually push it this far.

The mute turned her gaze back to Lalith. "I've never been raped either, if that's what you're getting at." The mute said this matter-of-factly, as if it were entirely appropriate observation. Lalith slid quickly back in his chair as if shoved. The mute took her finger, pointed it at the ground, and drew a circle in front of her. "Not in this vicinity anyway." The mute's voice didn't sound Sri Lankan; it was flat, accentless. He couldn't place the origin.

"Why would you say something like that," Lalith stammered. "Why mention *that* word?"

"What word?" the cat asked.

The mute nodded at Lalith the way someone might when coaxing information from a young child. "Tongue?" the mute offered softly. "Is that the word that offends you? Tongue?"

Lalith looked down at his hands. They were trembling. But why? The pair were only having a bit of fun with him. The cat, after all, was in some way a friend. He closed his hands so they formed fists. "I know what you read, about the army, in the papers . . ." His throat had begun to tighten involuntarily. It seemed to him he was frightened though he didn't know why or of what.

The cat smiled. "But I'm not the sort to do favors," she said in a high-pitched, singsong voice.

"But I'm feeling an onset of vapors," the mute sang in return.

The cat smirked. "That's *so* much more clever than mine."

The mute winked at Lalith.

"Be careful. I can have you both detained." Lalith tried to make this sound funny, as if he were in on their joke, but his voice pitched too high, the words attenuated. He appeared not playful or powerful but exposed, a playground bully unveiled for the helpless child he really was.

The cat brought a fluttering hand to her chest. "My goodness. Detained? For what? For childish limericks."

The mute clapped her hands. "That's so much more clever."

The women were mocking him, but he didn't know why. He started to feel as if he were floundering, almost helpless. He still didn't know if the mute were real. This odd conversation, ungoverned by basic rules of politeness, made the possibility to him even more unlikely. "Who are you?" Lalith whispered pleadingly at her.

The mute leveled her gaze at Lalith. "We're your ghosts," she replied, almost kindly. "Ghosts."

Lalith blinked. It was a riddle. "Ghosts? There's no such thing. Anyway, I don't believe in ghosts." But that wasn't true. His whole life he had served ghosts. He had built the Unicorn because of the ghosts of fallen comrades. Every battlefield was taken, ever decision to bomb a target was made, in the name of ghosts. Even now they kept the Tiger ghost entombed in his bunker to prove all the horror perpetrated had had a meaning. Why wouldn't these women be ghosts as well? But, in victory, didn't there have to be something real? He couldn't have fought for so long for nothing. Lalith stretched his hand toward the mute so that he could be sure, one sin for all, she was flesh and blood. She recoiled out of his reach.

The cat frowned at Lalith. She swatted away his outstretched hand and shook her head slowly. "Bloody hell, what's wrong with you, Lalith?" She paused. "She said we're your *guests*. What did you think? We *are* your guests. No?"

Lalith closed his eyes. A warmth crept up from his collar. When he opened his eyes the cat and the mute were staring at him curiously, almost as if they cared. Something had shifted—something in the atmosphere changed. Then he realized it was only the breeze wafting in, carrying with it the scent of bougainvillea.

The Major walked out onto the verandah, the other women following close behind. "I'm told dinner is ready," the Major said to Lalith.

Lalith leapt up at the sound of the Major's voice. When he did, he sent his chair tipping backward. It hit the ground with a clatter. The Major stared at it and then at Lalith with alarm. "Are you alright, sir?"

The cat gazed up at him expectantly. She held in her hands the now nearly empty teacup as if offering Lalith the dregs. The mute stared off. Her necklace glistened though the daylight was dimming and the servants had not yet turned on the overhead lamp. What was it the Tamil servant had said at the beginning? They had a new master. As Lalith remembered it now the servant had been speaking to the women. Lalith had misunderstood when he thought the servant was speaking to him. "If you would escort them to the table. I will be a few minutes." The Major nodded. He gestured at the women, and they stood and followed him inside without protest. Neither the cat nor the mute acknowledged Lalith as they walked past him. Lalith wondered if he had imagined the whole exchange, if he were slowly going mad, but there was nothing now except to continue to act as if he were in control.

When the women left the room, Lalith righted the fallen chair. He picked up the empty teacup. When he did, he noticed framed by the verandah railing and two posts the Unicorn, the one accomplishment of which he was most proud. It would be left to slowly rust there in the garden or in a shed somewhere. Lalith, soldier, military engineer, builder of bridges, walls, latrines, Unicorns now become museum curator. No, not museum curator. That had a noble ring to it. Cackling skeleton in a haunted house. That was more like it. Lalith sat on the chair, laughing to himself at the image, not caring how he might appear to anyone noticing him from inside.

The Chief Inspector's Daughter

A beggar recently discovered the bodies of four men and one woman in an SUV abandoned on the border of Colombo 8. The corpses' heads and hands were missing so that the victims could not be quickly identified. *Sri Lanka Daily* added, disapprovingly, that the woman had been posed in a provocative way, as if the body of a headless, handless woman could lure a man to sexual misdeeds. A rumor quickly spread: the victims were Tamils executed by the Sri Lanka army. We know, though few of us admit, our soldiers do such things. But I know, this time, we are all of us wrong.

I am drawn to these victims because I was there the night they were killed. Forsythia Lane, where the SUV was found, is one of the safer parts of the city. The lane is off the main street and is unpaved, nothing more then a pitted and potholed dirt road. With the recent bombings, it is one of the few places a seemingly empty parked car can remain unnoticed. And this is where my boyfriend and I drive when we want to make love.

We are both medical students at the University of Colombo and are still young, only nineteen. We both live at home. My father's servant, Saroja, lives in a small room beside our kitchen; she sees and hears everything.

There is no way for me to arrange for Siva to come to my house. But even if I were able to arrange it, I love my father and do not want to disrespect him in his home.

Instead, we pull the car to a stop under a large nag champa tree, the most romantic place on the lane. The yellow flowers shimmer and quiver in the night. Occasionally the breeze shears the blossoms from their stems, and a tumult of petals surrounds us. In those moments I'm reminded of a gift my American-born cousin gave me. A snow globe, she called it.

Siva and I were there under that tree the night of the murders. We were in the backseat of his father's car when Siva noticed headlights approaching. As the blades of light swept over Siva's back, the air went out of him, and his body rested heavy on top of mine. I nudged him away, propped myself on my elbows, and peered out the window in time to see an SUV and another smaller car pass.

After the cars were gone, Siva reanimated, as if a switch had flipped, and scrambled into the driver's seat. He backed down the lane without waiting for me to crawl into the passenger seat.

These victims, they cannot be completely innocent, no? If the killers were out solely to cause trouble and hurt Tamils, why had they not come to our car? Siva is a Tamil. They would have hurt him also, and me for being with him. But I do not say any of this. Since that night, Siva's behavior toward me has changed, and I know what he thinks: I am Sinhalese and I cannot be completely trusted.

The autopsy room at the university medical school has little more than a sputtering air conditioner to cool it. With the ten students that make up my class, as well as our lecturer, the room has become unbearably hot. I arrive a little late so that I don't have to go too far inside and can face the window. When the heat and the smell of the corpse become too much, I stare out over the tops of the king coconut palms and imagine the ocean somewhere in the distance.

The room is tiled from floor to ceiling. The tiles are aged and cracked; the grout is covered by a rust-colored mold. On an especially humid day condensation forms, and the walls appear to bleed. Reddish brown stains spread across the tiles. The room frightens some of the hospital workers, who put up quite a racket whenever they are told to go inside. They say the stains are the blood of the dead. Others say the room is possessed by the yakka.

Today we are autopsying a young woman. I look over at Siva. He is standing at the other end of the room, concentrating on what our lecturer is saying. I try to smile, but he pretends to be concerned about a fly buzzing near his face. He refuses to look in my direction. This is not unusual for him. He is a very good student, grateful for the opportunity to go to school and very serious about his studies. After lecture I try to make my way to him, but he is walking too far ahead.

It's only later that afternoon, as I'm waiting for the bus, that I see him studying with another student at the corner Barista's. Siva has his laptop out and is typing; his friend Ibrahim is reading the newspaper. We don't sit for our exams for another month, but Siva began studying at the start of the term; he studies every moment he can. I go in and slide into the booth next to him. Siva puts his arm around me and pulls me to him. His friend smirks as he watches us.

"Shouldn't you be studying also?" I ask Ibrahim.

He points to an article in the papers about the murders on Forsythia Lane. "My uncle and brother have a theory," he says to Siva. "This is a police killing." He brings his hand to his throat and makes a slicing motion. "My uncle says this is what the police do to you when you cross them." He looks at me slyly.

Siva purses his lips. "Your uncle talks nonsense, men." Ibrahim starts to protest, but Siva waves dismissively. "Go get another cup of coffee." Ibrahim seems reluctant at first but finally gets up and leaves.

I nestle into Siva. He is big, built thick and muscular. I am tall and strong, not one of the petite, slender girls—the pretty girls, they are called—so revered by Sri Lankans. But when I am next to Siva I feel fragile. He could crush my ribs with one firm squeeze.

The talk of the murders has reminded Siva of something. He tells me a white Peugeot had driven slowly by his parents' house yesterday. The same car returned and parked across the street for half the day.

Sri Lanka is a paranoid country. Twenty years of civil war makes us jump at our own shadows. Everyone has stories like Siva's. Stories of cars and vans that come in the day or in the middle of the night. He sees the disbelief in my expression.

"Sonali, we were there, at the place where they found the SUV. My father's car was there." I nod, but I do not want to urge him to think of that night. I do not want him to focus on the deaths of those people. "When those cars passed, maybe they could have belonged to the killers, no? Maybe they took down my father's license plate number."

I pull away from Siva and study the side of his face. "Those cars could have belonged to anyone. Maybe others have caught on, and they drive there for the same reasons we do." I try to give him a coy look, but he is staring into the screen of his laptop. "I will put a conversation to my father."

"No." Siva responds too quickly. "Tell your father nothing. He is unable to do anything."

"Of course he will do something. You do not have to worry about him finding out why we were there. I'll tell him a good story." Siva has pulled me tighter to him, but he is still not looking at me. Instead, he is hitting the escape key of his laptop, as if there is something wrong. "He will help anyone I ask him to help." I am sure of this, and I will Siva to have confidence in my ability over my father.

But he has gone pale, and I realize he is truly frightened. "Say nothing," he begs. "I am probably wrong about the car. It's nothing."

We speak English to each other because I do not know Tamil, and he does not speak Sinhala unless he must. There are other things that divide us—different gods, different history—but Siva and I also have at least one thing in common. I want to urge him to find somewhere else we can drive to. I want nothing more than to ease the burning I feel whenever I am near him. The pure physical need that overcomes me too often these days. But Siva slams his laptop shut and lets go of me. Unsure of what else to do, I straighten my shirt and run the palm of my hand over my hair. Siva packs away his computer.

When I return home, I open the front door and nearly step on a dead koi. There is a small fishpond near the veranda. The fish occasionally leap from the pond onto the porch. One of my father's dogs must have nudged it over to the entryway. I know there is a reasonable explanation, but after my conversation with Siva, I am disconcerted by what seems to me an omen.

I call the servant, Saroja. "Mokada, aney?" I ask. I try too hard to keep my voice from trembling. When Saroja sees the fish, she brings her hand up to the side of her face; her mouth forms an O. Her expression makes her look not unlike the dead fish. But as soon as this image comes to me, I feel sorry for conjuring it. Saroja is Tamil, and I have tried of late, since falling in love with Siva, to be careful how I think of Tamils. I tell her to go to bring a broom and a page of an old newspaper. She must hurry. My father will be back soon, and if he sees this he will be angry.

When my father returns from work, he is in a foul mood. He is the chief inspector at the Colombo 13, Kotahena, police station. He comes from a family of police officers. His grandfather was a constable in Panadura; his father was part of the team that investigated the assassination of Bandaranaike. My father is proud of his job, though it is at times dangerous. He has received death threats and even thought of retiring when my mother was ill, for her sake. But since her death he has only worked harder.

My father is tall and slim with dark skin the color of treacle. He is handsome; there are many women who come to the house with presents for him. Relatives have mentioned to him he should remarry. But even when my mother was alive, he kept to himself, talking little. He does not seem to miss her now. I have replaced her, and I am all that he needs.

He knows, since I am his only child, I will take care of him as he grows old. This is why he tolerates my relationship with Siva. He does not hate the Tamils and even argues they should keep Jaffna. But he also voted for the JHU and believes in the need to preserve the Sinhalese race. Because of me, he is friendly to Siva and his family. He sends Saroja to their house in a rickshaw carrying king coconuts or durian or rambutan if the fruit is in season.

My father is sitting on the veranda nursing his arrack and reading this morning's *Sri Lanka Daily*. He is so engrossed he barely notices when I offer him a plate of short eats. I look over his shoulder. I see he is reading an article about what the press has now dubbed the "SUV murders." The woman has been identified; it turns out she lived in Kotahena. I ask my father if he knows her. He shakes his head. Then I ask him if he has heard anything about the crime, anything particular about the bodies.

He talks to me often about his work, especially now that my mother is gone. But he peers into his tumbler as if he has spotted a bug. He asks me why I'm curious.

I try to laugh and make light of my inquiry. "I have an interest in dead bodies. I'm interested in pathology."

"Pathology," he scoffs. "This is not a job for women."

"I don't want to be any old lady doctor, patching scraped knees and easing stomach upsets. Pathology interests me. There are so many things that happen to the body after death. So many things you can tell about how someone lived." I know better than to speak with him when he is in one of his moods, but I'm carried away. "And also the possibility of helping to solve mysteries." I realize as soon as I say this that I have misspoken.

He laughs. "You are very young, no? Not even twenty." He picks out a meat patty from the plate of short eats. "Last week a man died after someone threw lye in his face. It is the boss of the restaurant he works at. No mystery. Three days ago a mother arrived at the station claiming her three-year-old son is being buggered. It is the stepfather. No mystery. When a husband is murdered, we arrest the wife. When a son is murdered, we arrest the father. There are no mysteries. There is nothing to solve." He finishes the patty and wipes his hand on a serviette.

"You, duwa, do not have the stomach for these things. Some women, yes. A woman who has lived a hard life. But not you."

He thrusts his tumbler toward me and asks me to refill it. When I lean forward to take the empty glass, he touches my forearm and looks up at me. He slurs a little as he speaks. "You are all that I have. You must do as I say." He pauses. "A girl like you should aspire to something noble. Working with children. Children will love you," he persists gently.

After dinner, after my father has gone to bed, I take the newspaper and find the article. The woman, the paper claims, was a known prostitute and petty criminal, frequently arrested. I wonder if my father tells the truth when he says he doesn't know her.

Siva calls in the morning. He is crying. His brother was copped the night before and is still being held at the police station. He wants me to ask my father for help. But before I can ring the Kotahena station, Siva phones and tells me his brother was released and is back home.

I try to call him later, but nobody, not even a servant, answers. Siva's family is rich, and they have a house in the Cinnamon Gardens, the wealthiest part of town. Even though it is hard now to find servants, his family has enough money to pay well. They have a cook and a gardener and even an ayah for Siva's youngest brother. There is always someone at his home, and I begin to worry. Why will no one pick up?

I don't see Siva again until the next morning. He is in a far corner of the university library. When I express my concern for him, he tells me what happened.

The family's cook had gone to the market in the late afternoon. As he made his way back home, two men on a motorbike tried to kill him. One of the men had held a cricket bat out as they passed, coming up from behind, riding at a high speed. The cook's legs were shattered, and he might never walk again.

"Someone wants to destroy my family," Siva whispers. The white

Peugeot, his brother's arrest, and now this. I want to remind him this is how things are here. If we hadn't been on Forsythia Lane, all these things could have happened anyway. Then Siva would have searched for any omen or any superstition. Now Forsythia Lane is the most convenient explanation for something that has no reason.

But I don't say any of this. I do the only thing I can. I tell Siva that I will ask my father to place a call to the Colombo 7 police station. He will talk to the chief inspector there.

Siva scowls. I can see the muscles in his jaw clench. I try to hold his hand, but he shrugs me off. "How is it you do not know?" He asks this question again and again without blinking or looking away.

I stare through the stacks of old books, mildewed and rotting in the heat. "Know what?"

Siva flips open his laptop and types my father's name. He begins to read.

Abdul Azeez lost use of his hands and arms after being hung by his wrists for forty-eight hours. Nihal Jayewardene disappeared. Last seen at the Kotahena station. Lakshmi Fernando gang-raped by three policemen at the Kotahena station house. Priya Jeganathan burned with a cigarette on her face, arms, and genitals.

Siva is about to go on, but I reach over and close the laptop. As I walk away, I teeter like I'm drunk. He does not call to me or come after me. I step out into the sun and am grateful for the scorching heat, so strong it makes me forget, for a moment.

Muslim/Sinhalese/Tamil/Burgher. UNP/LTTE/JVP/JHU/TNA. Royal/Thomian. There are too many choices. But still, they demand that I choose.

I am not a fool. I have heard the rumors about my father. It is impossible not to. But I know without asking how he explains what he has done. The rumors are all half truths and exaggerations by people who do not know how it is here. These people lead hard, desperate lives. They are brutal, and my father must talk and act using that same brutal language. This is the only way we can all be protected.

But I have never needed any explanations. I have never spent any time, until now, wondering what my father is capable of.

I do not go home. Instead, I wander the streets and then take a bus to Forsythia Lane. It is early evening and still light by the time I reach it, about seven o'clock.

I do not know what it is like for Siva, though I've tried to imagine. He told me once that swinging his legs out of bed, planting his feet on the clay floor beneath him, was not simply a physical act. It was a mental act, one propelled by urgency and single-mindedness. If he thought too hard, he would never leave his room. And every day something, sometimes something very small, nothing more than a loose word, made getting up the next day another nearly insurmountable obstacle.

No, I do not know what it is like to be that afraid.

From above me comes a piercing shriek, and the trees explode in a flurry of ripped leaves and broken branches: two mongooses fighting. Ahead of me a polecat noses through garbage left in the bushes. I consider turning around, but suddenly it seems important to move forward, to find what I've come here to see.

I approach the nag champa where Siva and I come. As I stand underneath, remembering our times here together, a man steps out from behind. In the remaining light, I can see he is old and stooped, with nothing but a tattered sarong to cover his body. Thick white hair, coiled like tiny watch springs, extends from his chest across his stomach. "Machchi, my children are dying," he hisses as he moves toward me, his palm extended. "My wife is dying." He smells of kasippu, the moonshine only the poor drink, and he speaks in heavily accented Sinhala, the way a Tamil might. His next words are all in Tamil, and I do not understand what he is saying.

Has he been living here all the time? Did he see Siva's car when we came here together? Did he watch us? Even though he smells as if he is drunk, his eyes are bright and alert, and he is studying me. He leans his weight on an old broom handle when he walks, but he can't mask his natural agility. It occurs to me he isn't really a beggar, but I still give him something.

I should turn back now. If I am hurt, people will have no sympathy for me. They will say I deserve it for coming here alone. They will say that because I am a chief inspector's daughter I believe I am untouchable, invincible. But this is not how I am. I am here only because I love Siva and my father, and I feel that there is something here, some proof that we are, all of us, innocent.

I walk down the lane without looking back. If I turn I will see the beggar standing straight, peering at me as I walk away. He will suddenly look younger and stronger. Once I've seen his true self, he will not allow me to leave. I walk on, aware now only of pushing my body forward, even as the lane grows dark.

I reach the cul-de-sac where the SUV was found. I expect something—markers, colored tape—but I see nothing to indicate a crime has taken place. Only a long wall that protects a derelict building and a cluster of aging forsythia bushes. It is dark now, but my eyes have grown accustomed. I can make out the form of things, but the ground around me is vast and regular and black. There is the warm breeze and the scent of jasmine. In the distance I hear the steady hum of motors and look behind me to see the headlights of two motorbikes approaching.

The bikes stop, and two men dismount. Though it is dusk, there is still enough light that I can make out their uniforms. One holds a torch, and they both have their hands to their waists. They are both gripping their batons; I know this without having to see. "Madame, what are you doing here?"

One of the constables moves quickly; he grips me by the arm. He digs his fingers into my flesh and pulls me close enough to him that I can smell the betel on his breath. I glimpse, for a moment, his stained, rotting teeth. The other holds the torch in my face so I am blinded.

But when I try to put my hand up to block the light, he exhales rapidly, a sound like air being let out of a tire. The man who is holding me moves away. He is being pushed back.

"Sonali," the man with the torch whispers. "Sonali, what is this?" He lowers the beam enough so that I can see his face. "Do you recognize me? Preshan." I nod. I have seen him before; he works for my father. Since I was a little girl, he has helped me find my father whenever I stopped by the station. He has even come to my house when my mother was sick.

The other constable is staring at his partner. "You know this person?"

"It's Sonali Gajaweera. Chief Inspector Gajaweera's daughter." The other constable looks at me, his mouth open. "What are you doing here?" he asks. This is not a demand but more a question of wonder.

I am emboldened by his meekness. "What are you doing here?" I ask him. "You are far from Kotahena." Anger flashes across his face, and he steps toward me. But Preshan is faster; he puts a protective arm around my shoulders and guides me toward the bikes. When I look back at Preshan's partner, he has his hands on his hips, and he is staring at the sky. When he approaches us, I can tell he wants to speak with Preshan, alone, but Preshan refuses to acknowledge him. "Leave us. I will take her home," he says.

Preshan watches as his partner's bike disappears down the lane. He turns to me. "What are you doing here, Sonali? It is not good for a girl to be out at night alone." Preshan's tone is soft, almost conciliatory. "Some people were murdered here."

"I know," I reply.

"Why are you here?" he presses.

I want to tell him about Siva, about how his family is being harassed. How Siva believes, how I believe, it is because of what we saw that night. How my father avoided speaking to me of the murders. Why would Preshan be here unless my father was involved? And if his men are involved, why would he not just tell me this when I had asked earlier? "Why are you here?" I whisper.

"We saw you walking up the lane alone."

I imagine the people in that report. Was it Preshan who burned that woman with the cigarette? Was it his colleagues who raped that woman? Where was my father for all of this? Or is it all lies? I cannot tell anymore. "They say those men were murdered by the police."

" 'They'?" Preshan scoffs. "They also say it is a military murder. They say it is a gang murder. Or schoolboys on drugs. They will soon say it is you, Sonali, if I do not take you home." He is about to walk to his bike when, suddenly, he swings the beam of light onto my face. I wince and try to look away. "What *are* you asking?" he demands.

I stand there, quietly. He sighs. "I will let your father know about your theories. Perhaps if he's in a good mood, he will share with you the truth."

He tells me to get on the back of his bike. I put my arms around his waist. As he starts slowly down the lane, I grip him tightly, pressing my body to his.

My father opens his wallet and gives Saroja a few rupee notes. I am standing to the side, next to the dining room table; he has refused to look at me since he and Preshan talked in the kitchen. Go to the market, he tells Saroja. Stay away for a little while, he adds. Saroja is reluctant to leave, but she is also afraid. My father and I stand quietly, both of us waiting until we hear Saroja dragging closed the metal gate that leads to the street.

When she is gone, my father slaps me. I have to brace myself against the table to keep from stumbling.

But he doesn't appear angry, only concerned. "Are you mad?" he asks. "Are you ill? You are walking in the street at night like a whore? Talking nonsense."

My cheek stings, and the pain makes me giddy. "I was there the night those men were murdered, thaththa. You need to tell your men that."

My father's lips tremble; his eyes narrow. Then his expression quickly returns to that of concern. "You're ill, duwa," he coos and makes as if to check my forehead for a temperature. "Let me help you, darling."

"Siva and I were there the night of the murders." My father looks confused. "You have heard his father's car was seen there, no? You were told the car was parked on the lane."

"What are you babbling?"

"But did you know *both* of us were there? Did your spies tell you that?"

"You are not feeling well. Come upstairs—"

"That was why his father's car was there. We were there so we could be together, thaththa." I take a deep breath. "You can leave his family alone now. You do not have to hurt them because they know nothing. We saw nothing."

My father is looking from my face to the floor and back again; his mouth is moving but no sound comes. "All rubbish," he finally mutters.

"The murdered woman was from Kotahena. A known prostitute, the papers call her. Arrested frequently. How could you not have heard of her?"

"How is it that you think I've met every prostitute in Kotahena?"

"A known prostitute? Your men are investigating? Why, thaththa? Colombo 8 cannot handle this case on their own?"

My father shakes his head. "I do not know what you mean. Who are *my* men?"

"Don't lie," I say this as calmly as I can manage. My father steps back, startled. "Why do you continue to lie? I recognized him. I recognized Preshan. I know he works for you." I pause long enough to catch my breath. "All the time you have lied, about everything."

He pushes me but not hard. It is a feeble attempt by someone who is angry but cannot do any harm, a schoolboy reacting to a taunt. I grip the edge of the table.

My father is standing, breathing hard, his head bowed. He is a guilty man. Or perhaps it is I who am the guilty one. "I know what you do," I say. My voice wavers and sticks to the back of my throat. "I've known for a long time," I croak, "all you have done to people." I let go of the table. I'm breathing hard, and I need a few seconds to catch my breath. "Siva says the police are harassing his family. If you are hurting him, if you are hurting Siva or his family, I will leave you." My father's eyes widen; he blanches. He is not angry now or concerned but scared. "You can die here alone. As you should."

This time he pushes me hard enough that I lose my balance. I do not black out when my head strikes the floor. I hear the cracking of my skull, but it does not sound as if it is coming from me. It is instead as if a bomb has ripped through my house. I curl up, tight, more from the pain than because I am afraid my father will hurt me. He leans over and whispers my name; he nudges me. I cannot respond or think. After a little while, I hear him walk away.

—————

I am still on the floor, my arms over my head, when Saroja and Siva arrive. Saroja cradles my head in her lap.

I ask them where my father, is but Siva ignores my question. Instead he tells me if I can move we need to go to the hospital. I try to stand on my own but feel dizzy as soon as I take my first step. I have to lean against Siva. We walk slowly to the street, and Saroja hails a three-wheeler.

Again, I ask about my father. Siva explains that neither he nor Saroja has seen or spoken to him. After my father told her to go, Saroja had taken a three-wheeler to Siva's. When they arrived at my house, my father's car was gone. They found me on the floor, unconscious.

At the emergency room, a lady doctor tends to me. She tells me I should stay the night. I have a concussion, and they want to make sure there is no, more serious, injury.

After she's left, Siva stays at my bedside. He brushes my hair from my face, and mops at my bruised face with a damp towel. Next to me a woman is screaming in Tamil, and I ask what she is saying. But he says not to worry.

As I look up at Siva, I wonder how long he has harbored this knowledge of my father. Has he always looked at me and wondered? Does he ask himself what I am capable of? I whisper to him that he should leave. He doesn't understand at first. He tells me Saroja called my aunt, and she will be here soon. I repeat myself, louder. I want him to go.

The pain is a screeching inside my head. The sound obliterates all my emotions and thoughts, and I can only close my eyes against it.

When I open my eyes again, I want you, Siva, not to be here.

When I awake, it is morning. My aunt is standing over me. The lady doctor is next to her. My aunt smiles and strokes the side of her face while the doctor explains how well I'm doing. But I'm not listening. Instead I'm searching the room, but Siva is gone.

—·—·—

Two weeks ago the inspector general released the identities of the murdered men: four Muslims who worked in the tea trade. A new rumor started to circulate: corrupt government officials had them executed. A few days later *Sri Lanka Daily* reported that two customs agents had been arrested. The murders were retaliation against a planter who refused to be extorted. The prostitute from Kotahena was, most likely, only a lure. An innocent bystander.

Next to the article were three photographs of the inspectors who worked on the case. I recognized all three: the Forsythia Lane beggar, Preshan, and Preshan's partner. The article also explained that Preshan had recently been promoted to his new post from the Kotahena department. This was his first major case.

I have not seen my father since that night. I live with my aunt now, my mother's sister, in Panadura, and I take the bus to school. My father does not speak to me, and I do not ask. I am aware that he sends money for me through Saroja.

I see Siva in the halls at university, but I always duck away before he can stop me. Finally he waits for me outside my classroom. He tries to explain how sorry he is. What to do, I tell him. I will never know what it is like to be afraid the way he is afraid, and he will never understand why I lived as long as I did with my father. He seems shocked at first that I would be so direct with him, and then he looks at me helplessly. I think of what the Lord Buddha has told us: when you see a drowning man, you should not help him. I have never understood this until now. It is too hard, in this moment, to reach for Siva and pull him to me. I am not strong, and it is better, much easier, to let him go. So I say the truth.

There is nothing we can do for each other; there is nothing more to say.

Pine

‹ ≡✦≡ ›

That year Lakshmi yielded and bought a Christmas tree. In sixteen years of living in the States and eight years of marriage, she
had never seen the need. If asked why, she explained this was a tradition with no place in her home. But now she could not keep one more
thing from Sareth and Aruni—not after everything they had lost. So
when Sareth, who was seven, asked for a tree, as he had for the past
three Decembers, she said yes. It was after all, only a pine tree with
decorations thrown on it. Still, karma has its effects, and, when she
recognized her uncle's voice on the phone, she felt as if he had caught
her out.

"Lakshmi, I need a favor," her uncle said. "The Sri Lanka Buddhist
Society has a priest from the temple in Atlanta coming for a daane.
He's flying into Raleigh-Durham this afternoon. I was supposed to
fetch him, but I'm on call tonight. Can't you pick him up, darling? He
can stay with you tonight, and I'll come by tomorrow morning."

"It's Christmas Eve, Vijay-mama."

"What's that got to do with you?"

"Is it okay for a priest to stay with me? Isn't it against his vows to
stay with a woman alone?"

"He's almost doddering, Lakshmi. I doubt he'll do anything to you, and I equally doubt you'll want to do anything to him. It's hardly fodder for a scandal. You have time for us, no?"

"I'm not trying to put you off. It's just that Nimal is coming tonight. He has some kind of request to ask in person."

"Isn't he your *ex*-husband now? Doesn't he have a new wife?"

"No, she's just his girlfriend."

"The priest is flying in at two. Won't that give you enough time?" He paused, "It will be good for Sareth to meet a priest. Don't you think?"

After they finished speaking, Lakshmi walked into the living room. In Sri Lanka the Christmas tree wouldn't have mattered to her. Every December, her parents had kept a small, plastic one on top of the refrigerator, and she had exchanged small Christmas gifts with some of her Christian friends. She had loved how the Colombo shopkeepers had decorated their facades with colored lights until the war put a stop to that. But here in America the Christmas tree seemed a time waster, an imposition of someone else's culture and tradition. Now, amid the devil-bird masks with hissing cobras wrapped around sharp beaks, the brass plates engraved and pierced with scenes from Sinhalese mythology, the batiks depicting dancers with arms flung wide and legs bent in traditional poses, the small pine tree—only a head taller than Lakshmi herself—looked out of place.

At the abandoned lot turned boreal forest, she had surveyed the felled trees tethered together and displayed like carcasses in a butcher shop and felt dismayed by the waste. When Lakshmi bought the tree, the salesperson informed her, after she had asked how she was supposed to make it stand, that she would have to purchase a tree stand, a tree skirt, and a humidifier to keep the needles from becoming brittle and dry. And she had to find decorations. At the local Kmart, she scoured rows of Santa Clauses, gaudily painted reindeer with red noses, crèches, and stars all which she deemed too holiday specific, before she settled on a box of silver and gold globes, tinsel, and colored lights.

She and Sareth decorated the tree while her two-year-old, Aruni, sat and watched, clapping her hands and reaching for the glistening ornaments. When they finished decorating, Lakshmi stepped back to assess their work. The tree sagged under the weight of its tinseled finery and with lights blinking—red, yellow, green, red, yellow, green—it lost any resemblance to its natural form. But Sareth didn't see it that way. Her heart tightened when she noticed him standing there, his dark, beautiful face radiant and warm like a piece of coal in a fire. He turned to her and smiled, "Amma, isn't it amazing?"

Two days later, he returned from school with a small package wrapped carefully in newspaper. He held it in front of him and walked gingerly, as if he were an unsteady waiter balancing a tray of glasses.

"What are you carrying?" she asked.

He held it out to her. "Open it, amma."

Lakshmi unwrapped the paper. A misshapen papier-mâché star, the size of her hand, covered in tinfoil and decorated with glass beads, lay inside. "What is this?"

"It's the star of Bethlehem. When I told Mrs. Pratt we got a Christmas tree she was so happy she helped me make it. She said that we have to wait and put it on top of the tree on Christmas Eve."

"You shouldn't have told Mrs. Pratt we have a tree."

"All the kids have Christmas trees," he beamed. "Now I'm like them." Lakshmi rewrapped the star and gave it back to him.

"Then why don't you keep it in your room until Christmas Eve." He wrinkled his nose. "Aruni will eat it. I'm going to keep it here, where everyone can see." He unwrapped the star and placed it on the middle of the kitchen table. After a few minutes consideration, he placed the newspaper wrapping underneath the star. So it would not get hurt, he told her.

She felt as if she lost him little by little each day.

—※—

That had been over a week ago. Now the tree looked even more pathetic. And, as if it were registering displeasure at its fate, a thin carpet of pine needles surrounded its base despite the stream of cool, moist air provided by the humidifier. She tried to keep the floor clean, but a new layer reappeared within minutes. There was nothing she could do about the tree now. She would just have to hope the priest would not notice it.

She took a back road to the airport to avoid holiday traffic. The rural landscape was barren and lonely; swaths of black and ochre stretched toward a sunless sky. A rare, early winter snow had fallen two nights earlier. Much of it had melted the day before and refrozen during the evening. A hard sheath covered the ground and trees. The patches of ice were cloudy and dense in the formless light of the gray December afternoon, and the landscape appeared trapped under a fragile coating of glass. As she drove, Lakshmi imagined reaching out and shattering the brittle world with just one warm touch.

Lakshmi arrived early at the airport so she could grab a smoke. She had tried to quit a couple of times since the divorce, without success. She had managed to reduce her habit to the occasional drag while sitting in the car just before work. The stress, however, of the impending visits by the priest and her ex-husband, Nimal, proved too much. The pack of cigarettes and the silver cigarette lighter with her initials engraved on the side—a gift from Nimal—now sat on the car seat beside her like faithful friends. She was not sure why she kept the lighter when she had packed up and stored everything else that reminded her of him. After months of trying to get her to quit, he had given it to her with the admonition that, if she were going to kill herself, she might as well do it in style—a bad joke. Still, the lighter reminded her of a time when they were able to laugh at each other's choices.

They had met during her sophomore year in college. Lakshmi had moved to the states when the Sri Lankan government closed the universities in order to crush student-led opposition. The shutdown, which was only supposed to last a few months, appeared as if it might, like the civil war, go on indefinitely. Her family had decided she shouldn't wait. So, at eighteen, she enrolled in a small college outside of Winston-Salem with the expectation she would go back home when she finished school.

In Sri Lanka, she had grown accustomed to the war; the fatalistic acceptance of a life attenuated by violence had become routine. But once in North Carolina, surrounded by the pristine Appalachian landscape, she had recognized the perversity in that existence. Then, she had met Nimal at a Sri Lanka Society party. A business student at Chapel Hill, Nimal had lived his whole life in the States, the child of immigrant parents who believed their son would succeed only if they pushed him to be as American as possible, without the influence from their Sri Lankan culture. When she met him, Nimal had just started to explore what he referred to as his roots.

When Lakshmi reached the terminal gate, the Buddhist priest was already waiting for her. She placed both palms of her hands together and started to drop to her knees. He stopped her before she could reach the floor. "It will make all these people jealous seeing such a beautiful woman kissing the feet of an old man."

The monk was tall and fleshy. Wire-rimmed spectacles balanced precariously at the tip of his bulbous nose; they seemed flimsy and ludicrously useless dangling in the middle of the priest's expansive face. He wore a black wool coat over his yellow robes; a black wool cap covered his shaved head. His left arm shielded a small bag that hung from his shoulder, and in his right hand he clutched a metal cane, though he did not seem to need it. In fact, he moved so quickly Lakshmi, who was much smaller, had trouble keeping up.

At her car, she opened the back door, but he waved his hand in protest and opened the front door instead. He paused when he noticed the pack of cigarettes and the lighter on the seat. Lakshmi reached around the priest and placed both objects on the dashboard. Great first impression, she chided herself.

—◦—◦—

During their marriage, Lakshmi created for Nimal an ideal of what it meant to be Sri Lankan. She cooked for him—kirri-bath, string hoppers, chapatti—all the food he had never tried. She took him to temple. Lakshmi described to him what it was like growing up in Sri

Lanka. What it was like to be an adult and to touch snow for the first time. Or how strange it was to have to listen to weather reports every day in order to know what to wear. When Nimal left, shortly after Aruni's birth, saying that maybe he had married too quickly, she felt he had not just betrayed his family and his culture, but now she felt she had to contend with her own betrayal. She was thirty-four, no country, no marriage, and remnants of a family. Were these losses the price she had to pay for her unwillingness to return?

After Lakshmi pulled into the garage, she sat wondering if she should help the priest out of the car. He made no move, so she got out and walked around to the passenger side, but as she reached for his door, the priest pushed it open quickly and she nearly fell. He was out of the car and almost to the house before she regained her balance.

Lakshmi steered him to the back door. She knew she probably would not be able to keep him from seeing the Christmas tree, but she did not want it to be the first thing he noticed. The priest, however, was more nimble than she expected. He slipped past her and made his way into the living room. He walked straight to the tree as if, somehow, he had known it would be there.

"Your husband is a Christian?"

"No swamin-wahanse. The tree is for my son. He's had a hard time this year, and he really wanted one."

"You're raising him a Buddhist?"

"Yes, but it's hard here. The temple is eight hours away. I try to teach him the prayers, but he's only seven. I saw no harm in letting him have a Christmas tree."

The priest remained silent for a few minutes. He supported one of the silver globes in the palm of his hand and rubbed his fingers across the silver veneer. The ghost of his thumbprint appeared on the shiny surface and slowly shrank away. Still holding the ornament in his hand, the priest said, "But you are the mother, no? You must set him on the right path. Buddhism is like the path on which we journey. We might feel tired and think that there will be no harm in stopping at an inn beside the path. But the inn is warm. The food is good. We may never leave, and then we will not reach our true destiny." A dry shudder shook the tree as the priest released the ornament; the piquant smell of pine needles exuded like a breath.

Lakshmi nodded, "Then swamin-wahanse, you will pray with us tonight? It will be good for my son."

"As you wish, I will pray with you and your family tonight. Your son and husband will be here soon?"

"My children are with a babysitter. She'll drop them off in a little while," she paused, "Swamin-wahanse, I'm no longer married, but my ex-husband is coming here tonight."

"No matter, we will still pray with him."

Lakshmi bowed her head further, "My ex-husband is coming with a friend."

"We will all pray."

"She is not Sinhalese."

The monk turned away from the tree. "This is a very American house, no?"

— ⚔ —

Lakshmi had come, now, to wonder if she had ever really loved Nimal or if he had simply represented a reason—a very good reason—not to return to Sri Lanka. Still, the divorce had been painful, and she very much wanted to ease the stress of it for Sareth and Aruni. She felt she gained nothing by keeping Nimal and his girlfriend from seeing the children. But when she opened her front door and saw them—Nimal and Wendy—standing so close to each other, her stomach dropped.

Wendy walked immediately to the tree, "It's beautiful!"

"I helped decorate it," Sareth said.

"Well, you did a good job." Wendy tousled Sareth's hair. He scowled and rubbed his hair flat with his hand.

"I thought you were against having one?" whispered Nimal.

Before she could answer, Sareth asked, "Dad, do you like it?"

"Dad?" asked Lakshmi, surprised. "He's your thaththi, Sareth."

Sareth looked up at her, eyes wide. "That's what the kids at school say."

"Your amma is right," said Nimal. "You should call me thaththi."

Wendy smiled and nodded. "That's okay, honey. In America we call our fathers all kinds of things." She winked at Lakshmi.

Lakshmi invited them to sit on the sofa. As he sat down, Wendy scooped Aruni into her arms and held the squirming girl firmly on her lap. Aruni's tiny hands reached for a silver cross dangling on a chain around Wendy's neck.

"No, no, sweetie," Wendy cooed as she gently separated Aruni's entwined fingers.

"That's pretty," said Sareth.

"Thank you. It's an early Christmas gift from your daddy." She corrected herself, "Your thaththi."

Sareth turned to Nimal, "Mommy got me three presents. They're in the hall closet. We're going to put them under the tree after," Sareth glanced at the bedroom and whispered, "*he* is gone."

Nimal gave Lakshmi a look. "Amma is giving you *three* presents? Really?" he said through a gritted smile, "How nice."

Aruni grabbed Wendy's necklace again.

"Let me take her." Lakshmi made a move toward them but Wendy waved her away.

"No, I'll just take it off." Still grasping Aruni with one hand, Wendy unlatched the necklace with the other and quickly caught it as it slipped toward her chest. She placed the necklace on the end table next to the sofa.

When she had first met Wendy, Lakshmi had noticed immediately the physical difference. Lakshmi was so small she bought her shoes in the junior miss section of the department store. Wendy was tall and athletic, with red hair and a round, pretty face. Tiny freckles like pin pricks covered pale, almost translucent skin.

Sareth told Wendy and Nimal about the priest staying in his room. They listened to him nodding as he described saying hello to the priest. Lakshmi was distracted from their conversation by the sound of doors opening and closing in another part of the house. She got up and walked to the kitchen. The priest stood next to the kitchen table. He wore a long, dark cardigan over his saffron-hued robes.

"Swamin-wahanse, can I get you something?"

"It's time to pray," responded the priest. "I will pray with you and your son in the sitting room."

"My son will sit with you now, and I will join you once my guests leave."

Lakshmi returned to the next room and explained to Nimal and Wendy they would have to move to the kitchen.

"We're not planning to stay long," replied Nimal. Wendy touched his arm lightly and he continued, "We have a favor to ask you."

Sareth took Wendy's hand in his and looked up at her. "Can I sit with you in the kitchen?"

"Let's ask your amma," Wendy answered, looking at Lakshmi for approval.

"No, putha," Lakshmi pulled Sareth and steered him toward the middle of the living room, "you need to stay here and pray."

"Do I have to?"

"Yes." Lakshmi tried to control her voice, aware of Nimal and Wendy watching her. "Sit on the ground in front of the sofa and keep your sister on your lap. Listen to what the priest tells you."

With a loud huff, Sareth slumped on the floor. The priest, who had been listening in the doorway, came and sat with them. He leaned forward and started to speak softly to the children.

⊷‧━✦━‧⊷

In the kitchen, Lakshmi turned to Nimal. "Before I forget. Can you help me put this on top of the tree?" Lakshmi started to show Sareth's star, but it was no longer on the table.

"That's strange. Sareth made an ornament for the top of the tree. Now it's gone."

"Maybe he took it to his room," Nimal suggested. "We'll ask him about it in a minute. But first I have a favor to ask. I'm going to be baptized two weeks from now. That's a Sunday when you have the kids. But I'd like them to be at the baptism."

"You're what?"

"Wendy's family is coming and I would like it if Sareth and Aruni could be there. It's an important day for me."

"You're converting?"

"Amma, Aruni won't sit still." Sareth stood in front of them holding Aruni's hand. Lakshmi pulled Aruni onto her lap.

"Go back and sit with the priest," she told Sareth.

"I don't like him. He's weird."

"Don't talk like that about a priest, putha."

"That's right, Sareth. A priest is a holy man. You should show him respect," explained Nimal.

"Do it for me. Won't you?" Lakshmi asked gently.

Sareth pulled on Nimal's sleeve and pleaded, "But he smells funny."

Lakshmi felt her face grow warm. "If I hear you say anything like that again, no television for a week." She grabbed Sareth by his shoulder. "Listen to me! You're never to say bad things about a priest. Now go back and sit down!" Aruni hid her head against Lakshmi and started to fuss. Sareth stood staring at Lakshmi, blinking. He turned to go.

"Sareth," Nimal stopped him. "Your amma said you wanted me to put your star on the tree. Do you have it?"

Sareth bit his bottom lip and pointed to the table. "I put it there."

"Putha, please? Just tell the truth."

"It's okay," said Nimal. "Go sit with the priest." Sareth hunched his shoulders and walked slowly away.

As Nimal turned to watch Sareth leave, the light struck the convex surfaces of his glasses, making them white and opaque. Nimal nervously crossed and uncrossed his long, thin legs before turning back to Lakshmi. "I'm sorry, I didn't think this would upset you so much, but this is important to Wendy and me."

"Sareth is confused enough as it is."

"Look it's not like this doesn't happen all the time in Sri Lanka. Think of all the people you know who are raised in mixed families."

"That's different. They live in Sri Lanka. Sareth has to have some grounding, Nimal. You can't just push and pull him at will."

They sat staring at each other, the only sounds the faint electric hum of the refrigerator and the rustle of fabric as Nimal continued to cross and uncross his legs. Wendy leaned over and placed her hand on Nimal's arm, "Okay honey, let's go." To Lakshmi she said, "I'm sorry. This was a lot to put on you. We don't want Aruni or Sareth to become Christian."

"We?"

"I have respect for your culture. I think it's beautiful."

Lakshmi turned to Nimal and said, "You ask too much."

"Wendy is right. We'll go now, but please think about it."

Lakshmi buried her face in Aruni's hair without answering.

———— ❊ ————

A light rain began to fall. Lakshmi tried to dodge the chilly drops as she walked to her car. She slipped into the front seat, closing the door so that she could sit in the cold, crisp darkness. While her eyes were still growing accustomed to the dark, she reached for the cigarettes and lighter on the dashboard, but then drew her hand back in surprise. She switched on the car light. The pack of cigarettes was there but the lighter was gone. She felt carefully along the dashboard and checked under the seat. After a few minutes of searching, she decided to wait until morning, when there would be enough light to see. She sat back and closed her eyes.

She thought about Sareth and wondered what he'd done with the Christmas ornament. He held so much inside himself; she could see it in the tightness of his mouth and stiffness of his small shoulders. He had been having trouble at school lately. Some older students had taunted him. Sareth had pushed one of them before the teacher could intervene. The teacher apologized to Lakshmi, assuring her no disciplinary action would be taken against Sareth. She also told Lakshmi she was planning a special class to teach the students about the cultures of India and asked if she would like to make a presentation. We are from Sri Lanka, not India, was all Lakshmi could think to respond. Sareth refused, even when she pressed him, to talk about the incident. And after a while she stopped trying to talk to him about it, afraid to push him too hard and wondering why he would not trust her more.

The next morning Lakshmi was sitting in the kitchen, cradling a cup of coffee, when she heard the crunch of gravel as a car rolled to a stop on her driveway. She looked out the kitchen window, expecting to see her uncle. Instead, it was Nimal. She opened the kitchen door for him as he walked up to the house. He came in shivering and blowing into gloveless hands. Lakshmi closed the door behind him.

"Look, first I want to apologize for last night," Nimal offered. "I should have come on my own, but Wendy likes the kids and she wanted to see them." Nimal laughed nervously. "Also Wendy left her necklace here last night. I just wanted to pick it up for her."

"I haven't seen it."

"She said she left it on the end table in the living room."

Lakshmi led Nimal into the next room.

"It's not here."

Nimal dropped to his hands and knees and looked under the sofa. He stood up shaking his head.

"Maybe Sareth saw it." She called to Sareth, who came running from the back of the house. When he saw Nimal, he ran and hugged him. Nimal picked him up and sat him on the sofa.

"Sareth, Wendy left her necklace here. Have you seen it?" asked Nimal. Sareth bit his lip and shook his head slowly.

"We won't be angry. Just tell the truth."

"We know you just took it to put it some place safe."

"I didn't take it!"

"Then, putha, who else could have?"

"The priest took it!"

Lakshmi crouched in front of Sareth and looked up at him. "I'm not mad. Just tell the truth."

"I am telling the truth," Sareth whined. "The priest took it. I saw him put it in the pocket of his sweater."

"If you saw the priest take it, why didn't you say something earlier?"

"You said you were going to punish me if I said anything bad about the priest."

Lakshmi sat back, resigned. Sareth was lying now and of all things about a priest. One more thing to add to the list of all that could go wrong. As if realizing the significance of a detail half noticed from the corner of her eye, she turned and looked at the tree.

There was a bare space among the branches—a space where a silver ornament once hung. Sareth followed her gaze. "He took something from the tree didn't he?" he asked.

Lakshmi nodded, "Alright. I'm not going to punish you. But go to my room and wait for me. I have to finish talking to your thaththi." Sareth pushed himself from the sofa and ran off.

"What the hell just happened?" Nimal asked.

"My lighter is gone and the priest was the only one in the car. The star is gone and the priest was in the kitchen last night. He was in the living room alone when Sareth came into the kitchen."

"You're kidding me," Nimal groaned. "What am I going to tell Wendy?"

"Wendy? What am I going to tell Sareth?"

"He's just a kid. He'll get over it. But Wendy really liked that necklace."

"Why don't you go confront the priest? Maybe you can wrestle the necklace from him."

Lakshmi stood up and walked back to the kitchen. Nimal followed behind. "Look, I'll figure out something to say to Wendy. But now won't you at least consider letting them come to the baptism?"

Lakshmi stood swung around. "What do you mean 'now'? You'll lie to Wendy if I give in to you? Protect our family honor? Protect our cultural honor? Or maybe this proves they should be Christian."

"That's not what I'm saying!" Nimal exclaimed, palms open. "I just want them to be there. They're my family."

"What about them? What about not confusing them?"

"Lakshmi, you don't know what it's like. To get ahead in this country you have to fit in. No one notices everything that's the same about you. Just what's different. My job is closed unless I try to fit in. These guys I work with. They actually make deals at church socials."

"You're converting so you can advance your career?"

"No, I'm converting because that's the world I live in. My friends. My coworkers. Wendy. Wendy is very important to me. I want to share my life with her, and her religion is important to her. I personally don't care what religion I am. Hell, it's more of a sham to pretend I'm a Buddhist just to make a point."

"What are you going to tell Sareth when he asks?"

"I'll tell him the truth. I thought it was the right thing to do."

"For Wendy?"

"Yes, for Wendy."

She leaned against the edge of the kitchen counter to steady herself. "What does this say to our children?" she asked softly. "What does this tell them about who they are?"

"Lakshmi, you're not the only one who loves them. You're not the only one who understands them. I do know what they're going through. Has it ever occurred to you I know that better than you?"

"You should go." She opened the kitchen door. Outside, he turned to her and asked, "Seriously, what do I tell Wendy?"

"Tell her what you really think. Tell her you can't trust *those* people." She slammed the door and locked it. She kept her burning forehead against the cold wood long after Nimal's footsteps died away.

Her uncle handed Sareth and Aruni two small packages. Trinkets, he told Lakshmi when she stared at him. "It is only a holiday," he mused as they watched the two children run gleefully into their rooms to unwrap their presents. Her uncle stared at the Christmas tree for a few seconds before sitting down on the sofa.

"Don't say anything, mama."

Her uncle shrugged. "I've always thought the trees were quite lovely, like the Vesak lanterns. I'd have one if Nalini didn't think they were a major nuisance." He sighed. "One of my friends—a Jewish chap—never had a Christmas tree growing up in Brooklyn. He has a Christmas tree now. You know the reason the bugger gives? He's afraid his patients are going to drive by his house, see he doesn't have a Christmas tree and stop coming to him. It's pointless being afraid of such things. You should do what you want and be happy," laughed the uncle. "The priest gave you no trouble I hope?"

"Well—"

"Very sad life, that one. His family gave him to the monastery when he was a boy because they were too poor to feed him."

"That seems sad—to have that choice made for you."

"Still, what a hardship his life would have been without the monastery."

"Nimal is converting, mama."

"Is that so? All that glisters."

"He must love her very much." An emptiness tugged at Lakshmi's chest as she said these words.

"There's nothing you can do about that."

The priest came in followed by Sareth, who was holding Aruni's hand. Lakshmi's uncle kneeled and bowed his head to the ground at the priest's feet. After her uncle stood up, Lakshmi worshipped the priest as well. As she bowed, she heard her uncle tell Sareth to do the same.

She watched from the corner of her eye as Sareth knelt in front of the priest; he looked, for a moment, just like a little Sri Lankan boy. As Sareth sat up, Lakshmi smiled and winked at him. He smiled bashfully in return.

As her uncle was leaving, he put his arm around her shoulder and kissed her on top of the head. "You're coming to the daane? It will be good for the children to see."

"Of course, Vijay-mama. I will come."

By the time they returned from her uncle's home three days later, the tree had begun to turn brown. Lakshmi sent Sareth and Aruni to her room to watch television. She started by taking the ornaments of the tree and placing each one carefully in its original box. After she was done, she took the boxes, the tinsel, and the lights and crammed them deep inside the hall closet. She pulled the tree of the stand. Pine needles pricked at the skin revealed between her coat and gloves as she dragged the tree outside.

When she reached the garbage cans, she caught her breath and stared at the tree at her feet. Despite the bare patches where the needles had fallen away, it was again a simple pine tree, sheared from its roots and resting on its side. She pulled it up and balanced it carefully against one of the cans. With her foot, she arranged the gravel and dirt around the base. After she was finished, it looked, at a cursory glance, as if it had been planted there. Now, she mused, the tree would exist again, for a short time, as it had once meant to be—a reprieve, even if it were only an illusion.

The Other One

E laine stepped back from the crease and started her run, elbows bent. She arced her arm for the delivery, her wrist twisted slightly, and she released the ball. The ball hit the pitch and angled toward the batsman. Elaine had bowled a surprisingly aggressive line and length for—well, I'll be honest here—for a woman. The batsman misjudged the height and speed of the ball, stepped back and rested her weight on her back foot. She missed. The ball hit off stump and the wicket collapsed, reduced to a pile of sticks.

I turned to my daughter, amazed. "Did you see that?"

"Yeah, that's why I brought you," my daughter replied. Mythri played on a junior women's cricket team and Elaine had been hired to help teach her team spin bowling. They'd worked together for a few weeks now.

Elaine turned and smiled at the captain of her team, a smile that conveyed both bravado—I knew I was going to do this—and relief— thank god I did it. I knew that feeling well: the adrenaline rush of accomplishment and skill. The fielder at mid-off threw her arms around Elaine. Her other teammates high-fived her. The batsman mouthed a congratulations in Elaine's direction. Cheers and applause roiled through the stands.

"But, she just bowled a . . ." I stammered, ". . . on *that* pitch . . ."

My daughter turned her petal-shaped face to mine and wrinkled her nose. "Exactly, appa. Like I said, that's why I wanted you to see her play."

Out on the field the next batter took position. The new batsman appeared nervous. She struck her bat hard against the dirt and positioned her feet. Even through all the padding, I could tell she was solidly built. She gripped the bat high up. This was a batsman capable of playing real shots, not just sweeping the ball. But, beneath, the helmet I could see she was blinking too much.

Elaine King's competitors were afraid of her.

"Introduce me to her, after the game."

My daughter, Mythri, nodded slowly. "Yeah, but the only thing is, you can't . . ." She hesitated. "You can't hit on Elaine, appa. She's, like, my age."

My daughter was fifteen. Elaine looked to be in her late twenties. They were nowhere close in age. I didn't really hit on women—never in front of my daughter. I'd been on a few dates since the divorce, and it was Mythri's mother who had ended the marriage.

More than that, I considered Elaine an athlete capable of doing something fairly astounding. I had only wanted to tell Elaine I respected her ability, and it bothered me that my daughter would see anything other than that. I also knew Mythri was a girl who had lost a lot: a mother and father to divorce and the sense of unit that an intact family gives you. I guessed she was really worried about losing me yet again.

The batsman stepped forward from the crease and with a quick, forward defensive stroke sent the ball rolling through a gap in long off. It hit the boundary. The umpire swept his hand from side to side signaling a four. Elaine turned and smiled broadly. She enjoyed the game no matter if she bowled the opponent out or if they scored. It was the beauty of cricket that mattered.

"Daughters do not talk about these things with their fathers. It's absolutely inappropriate," I whispered.

After the game, at my request, my daughter texted Elaine. We finally spotted her in the parking lot, looking for us. Mythri ran up to her, me jogging behind. She spoke to Elaine before I got there. Just as I reached them Elaine offered me her hand declaring that she'd heard a lot about me. She spoke with a pronounced Southern drawl which surprised me. I hadn't asked Mythri where Elaine was from and had assumed, since she played cricket so well, that she was English or Australian.

Elaine's grasp was firm and warm, and she held my hand just a second too long. I leaned in and said to her, "I want you to meet the boys." She shook her head at me, confused. "If you don't mind, I'd like you to meet my team." I was the captain of the Edenboro Warriors. Our team represented the Edenboro regional cricket club. "Maybe you'd even consider bowling at some of our practices."

She brightened and I sensed something in her unfold, that miraculous thing that women do that always, no matter the age or the physical attractiveness, swallows me whole. My daughter tensed. She tugged at my sleeve, but I ignored her. I loved my daughter. She ruled my day-to-day life. But Cricket was God. I didn't take my eyes from Elaine. She was the best spin bowler I'd met in a long, long time, and that was all that really mattered.

⊷—⊏⊏⊹⊐⊐—⊶

My team, the Edenboro Warriors, was an eclectic group representing nearly eleven nations. We even fielded two American players, men who had spent time in England and Australia and learned to love the game. We were a good team, and we probably had the best seamer, Sahid Chamkanni, in the region. But we were lacking spin. Our best spinner had recently relocated with his family to the Research Triangle and had begun playing for one of the opposing teams. We were lucky in Edenboro to have solid players. But Edenboro, North Carolina isn't exactly overflowing with cricket talent. That was why Elaine was so important.

I arranged for her to meet a group of us—Sahid, who was also my vice captain, and four other players—at a local restaurant. Sahid was already there at the bar with one of our batsmen, Andrew Cummings, a Southerner who had picked up cricket while a Rhodes scholar.

When I approached the bar I saw that the two men were both huddled together looking at Sahid's iPhone. On his phone was a photograph of a woman. She was standing in front of a mirror, nude. "My lab partner," Sahid informed me. "She sent this to me. I've talked to her a handful of times." I pushed the phone away without looking. "I didn't ask her to send this," he insisted. "I didn't even hint I wanted to see her naked."

Sahid was probably the best-looking man I'd ever met. Tall, olive-skinned with black curly hair. I was amazed at the number of women who threw themselves at Sahid, really hurtled themselves in his path. But unlike a lot of physically beautiful people I've known, Sahid wasn't particularly invested in his good looks. He'd grown up in a conservative Muslim community in Charlotte before moving to Durham to study at Duke. He was intelligent and serious and focused and flummoxed by all the attention he received from women. He told me once that he didn't believe those women saw him. They only saw what they wanted—the status of being with the best looking guy in the room, dating the soon-to-be-doctor. I remembered liking him a lot in that moment, even admiring him for being bothered by that recognition.

Sahid started clicking through what appeared to be a series of photographs taken by this woman. Andrew gawked. Another man at the bar, a stranger to us, had sidled over and craned his neck. Sahid shook his head and frowned.

I put a hand on Sahid's arm. "Machan, delete the photographs."

Andrew started to protest. I wagged a finger at him. "Bugger it, men. This meeting is important, the best chance our team has, and we're all going to behave." The last thing I wanted was for Elaine to see us acting like a bunch of first class assholes.

I spotted Elaine coming through the front door of the restaurant. She was wearing a black sundress and sandals. She wore her long hair loose around her shoulders. The self-possession I had noticed out on the field had morphed into gracefulness. I glanced at Sahid and Andrew to see if they had noticed her too, but they were still staring at Sahid's iPhone. I snatched the phone and held the off button until the screen went dark. Elaine stopped and said something to the hostess who pointed in my direction. I waved. "Your conversation ends now," I hissed at both of them as I returned Sahid's iPhone to him.

The other two teammates arrived shortly after us, and we all gathered at a table near the bar. Elaine told us a little about herself. She had started tennis at a young age and played tennis and basketball in high school. She had gone on to play tennis for her university but had given up a serious career to focus on her studies. Her father was Australian and had loved cricket. He'd shown her how to play and shown her how to spin bowl. But she hadn't started playing seriously until a few years before.

"Sebastian here says you're good," Sahid observed. "Spinning isn't something you suddenly pick up in your twenties."

"Like I said, I played since I was a kid. And I'm a good athlete, I guess."

Elaine wasn't a pretty girl. Her face was a bit too long and horsey. She was big-boned and muscular. But there was a real energy, a drive, to her. I knew Sahid and Andrew well enough by now to know that each of them had already estimated her cup size. Raj was so painfully and deeply married I wasn't sure he saw women any more. But whatever my teammates were really thinking about her they weren't letting on to Elaine. This meeting was cricket.

Elaine paused and took a deep breath. She looked down at her beer as if embarrassed. "I can show you something," she offered. She shifted her weight in her seat, then extended her arms in front of her and held her hands, tips of fingers nearly touching. She took her left hand and placed it against her right palm. She pressed down so that her hand bent at the wrist. Elaine's hand passed a ninety-five degree angle. She kept going. Eventually, she removed her left hand but her right continued to move until the back of her hand easily rested against her forearm. It looked terribly painful, and I couldn't help but flinch. Elaine didn't even blink.

Sahid's eyes widened. Andrew's expression flickered somewhere between awe and aversion. Beside me Raj gasped. "The ghost of Murali lives in you," he murmured. Murali, the greatest spin bowler who has ever lived, wasn't dead. He was retired, though, from cricket, which to some of us was the same thing.

"That's a pretty neat trick," Sahid whispered.

"It isn't a trick," Elaine replied. "It isn't even an ability. It's a genetic malformation."

"Like an X-man," Sahid offered.

"But it's also the reason I can spin the ball so well," Elaine said.

"Look, we need another spin bowler for our team," I explained. "And you *are* good. I have to check the bylaws, but if a woman can play I think we could use you." It was my turn to be gaped at. But no one protested either. They were all of them too gentlemanly to do so in front of Elaine, and probably they had been rendered speechless by Elaine's demonstration of extreme flexibility.

Sahid pointed at her. "Can you do that with your left hand?" he demanded. She looked at Sahid then, and registered him. I could see it in her face—the recognition of how good-looking he was. I admit I felt a bit disappointed.

She explained to us she could bend her wrist in the other direction but couldn't quite touch her fingers to her forearm. She demonstrated for us. "Cool," Sahid said, nodding his head with real admiration. "Completely fucking 'A' cool." I smiled at Elaine. She smiled back and I felt a tug at the base of my stomach. Beside me, Andrew offered to buy her another drink.

<hr />

It was easier than I thought to get Elaine on to the team. The president of the club protested at first but then when I mentioned to him the potential publicity it might generate—a Southern woman playing for an all male, mostly immigrant club—he backed off. The vice president made some half-hearted attempt at protest: some nonsense about there being no locker rooms and so on. Except at the venues we played—community parks and university grounds—there were always women's locker rooms.

Cricket isn't a sport that favors size or physical strength alone. Certainly it can help to be big and powerful, but the greatest batsman to ever play the game—outside of Donald Bradman—is Sachin Tendulkar. He's 5' 5" and slight. Cricket is a game of physical elegance, wits, and intelligence. There are myriad variations on any form of bowling, on any batting stroke.

Cricket is also a great equalizer. Most Americans when they think of cricket think of men in white running leisurely across fields of grass. It's a game of colonials. That's not true anymore. It's our game now—the Subcontinent's. We've taken it and made it our own. We've invented a style of batting. We've reinvented bowling. The English now have to come and play our game if they want to prove they're any good. I still remember the thrill I felt the day that Tony Greig realized what the Pakistani wicketkeeper Moin Kahn was saying to the Pakistani spin bowler Saqlain Mushtaq. "Use the 'doosra.'" Use the 'other one.' A South Asian, one of us, Saqlain Mushtaq had invented a whole new variation of an athletic skill that was nearly three hundred years old.

And it was that equalizing effect that allowed Elaine to fit in right away. I was surprised how quickly the boys accepted Elaine. No one grumbled when I told them, not a protest. We wanted to be good. Elaine would get us there. Each of us came to admire her. Unlike Raj, whose ability to tell time had not made it with him past the Greenwich Mean, Elaine showed up to practice at the designated hour. She listened when people offered her advice. Unlike Andrew, who appeared to be texting his girlfriend instead of fielding, and Sareth, who was too fat to run anywhere, she actually went after the ball. Her one fault was that she seemed a little too serious—tough physically and too determined emotionally. One day a bouncer clocked her in the head during batting practice. The sound of the ball hitting her helmet was loud enough to be heard past the boundary. I wanted to take her to a doctor or at least let Sahid examine her, but she refused. She remained at the wicket and didn't even take a water break.

This determination intimidated the other men, and it shamed some of the less dedicated players. I tried to broach the subject with her. When I encouraged her to have a little more fun, she narrowed her eyes. "My father told me if I wanted to play on the same level as men, I had to do everything better. Bowl better. Bat better. Take the pain." As a child I'd been taught to treat everyone with respect and compassion, but I admit now that it's only in the past few years that I've paid attention to the ways this world humiliates women. From the Bratz dolls that Mythri used to play with to the war photographs of Tamil women from villages not very far from where I grew up stripped naked, legs splayed, genitals exposed raw and bleeding, bullets holes in their foreheads. Only a year before, Sahid had turned to me and said: "The only monogamous woman is one who fears God." At the time, I had patted Sahid's shoulder and said "Machan, that might have been true for another time, in another world. But not here, not today." We were all of us trying to work our way out of some darkness. I didn't think what Elaine's father had told her was right, but I admired the strength it gave her. I didn't mention my concern again.

The day of Elaine's first match, we won the toss, and I elected to bat. It was hot and dry, and I thought if we could put enough of a total on the board they'd have to chase us. Things were going well from the start. Our two best batsmen, Patel and Jerry, were taking good shots, not hitting any loose balls, really judging each ball on its merit. Then Patel was hit in the shin pads. The opposing team wanted an LBW called and tried to appeal. In the middle of the chaos, Jerry took it on himself to try to steal a single, but Patel wasn't ready to run. The opposing team's fielders were paying attention and there was Patel caught halfway, between two wickets, flailing. He was easily stumped.

Next up to bat was Sareth. He was fat but a good batsman capable of elegant shots that scored our team big numbers. He was an immigration lawyer and his firm was also the team's biggest source of financial support. They'd even provided three cheerleaders decked out in the team's colors, "Khan, Kuralt, and Klein 4Immigration 252-865-0021" stenciled across the backs of their uniforms. The opposing team's wicket keeper was from the Australian school of sledging and was capable of being a royal, Grade A asshole. He was always getting on Sareth for his weight. I counseled Sareth to keep his head, and so far he had managed. But as he walked up to the wicket, swinging his bat back and forth, the opposing team's wicket keeper called to him, "That's a very small bat for such a big man."

Sareth kept his eyes trained on the dirt. He clenched his jaw and kept on moving. "I mean what does the size of a man's bat say about him? Or you know, come to think of it, maybe the bat's normal and it's you that's too fat," Sareth didn't respond. The wicketkeeper wasn't letting it go. "I mean seriously how does a bloke who fucking plays a sport like this one get so fucking fat. Too much jerk chicken?"

Sareth stopped at the wicket. He pulled his shoulders back and leveled his gaze at the wicketkeeper. I knew what was coming even before Sareth said it. I sprung forward but was only halfway to him when he rolled back his shoulders, tilted his chin, and began to intone: "I am fat, my dear sir," he paused for effect, "because every time I fuck your wife she throws me a biscuit." It wasn't an original insult, but it had its intended effect. The wicketkeeper took a step toward Sareth, fists balled. Sareth dipped his head, rounded his shoulders, and body slammed the wicketkeeper. The opposing team's fielders were running toward the two men. Jerry hurtled his own rather lean frame into the brouhaha.

Ten minutes later, after we had iced Jerry's freshly blackened eye, forced Sareth off the wicketkeeper, agreed to eject the wicketkeeper from the game for unsportsmanlike conduct, we commenced play. Everyone promised to behave. I looked over at Elaine who was seated on the bench staring at us. She hadn't gotten up to help break up the two men, and she was watching us now with a grim expression, her arms folded.

Despite all that diversion, Elaine ended up doing very well for us. She was the second highest wicket taker after Sahid, and she held her own. As we celebrated hugging each other and slapping each other on the back I noticed she stood a little ways from the rest of us. The men were shaking her hand and congratulating her but she was a woman, and most of the men were married or had girlfriends and felt reserved around her.

I was about to go up to her and invite her to go out for drinks with the rest of the team when I saw Mythri and some of her friends run past me to Sahid. They gathered around him, each of them bouncing and straining to get his attention. Mythri fluttered her eyelids at him and gave him a coy smile. I gawked at them. When had that happened? This interest in Sahid? As I stared, one of the girls handed him a pen and chirped about how they were big fans of his. They held out their arms to him. Would he autograph their hands for them? I was about to put a stop to this when Elaine nudged me. "Great game," she said. She studied my expression. "You look upset?"

I nodded at the girls.

Elaine laughed. "I think it's harmless and Sahid knows how to handle himself."

I noticed Mythri touch Sahid on the forearm. Sahid looked at her for a moment, then, glanced at me. He took a step back, away from my daughter.

"The boys are going to celebrate," I said to Elaine. "I'll be late because I have to take Mythri to band practice." Her sweat had dried, forming ashy bands of salt along her hairline and little bands across her neck. Her hair was mussed and tangled and sweat stains had formed at the armpits of her uniform t-shirt. She looked an entirely physical being—a woman of muscle and strength—and sexy. My neck grew warm, and I hunched a little in embarrassment.

She said, "Sure, I'll hang out. Sahid will be going, right?" My stomach gave a sharp twist. I told myself it was entirely natural—they both had a lot in common—but I also felt jealous. Was it possible she was interested in Sahid as well?

Elaine brought fingers to mouth and gave a loud, sharp whistle. Sahid looked up with something like desperation in his face. "Sahid, Sebastian and I want to talk to you. In private," she called. Sahid seemed so relieved I thought for a second he might start crying. When he reached us, Mythri broke away from her friends and ran over to us. Elaine tried to say hello to Mythri. She glared at Elaine and then turned her back to her. A week ago Elaine was Mythri's hero. Now, she couldn't even say hello. Mythri grabbed my hand. "We have to go, appa, or I'll be late." I nodded and said my goodbyes to Elaine and Sahid.

As we crossed the field, I admonished her, "Why were you so rude to Elaine?"

"Doesn't she get enough attention from you? Does the whole family have to get into the act?"

I stopped her. "What are you talking about?"

Mythri took a sharp whistling breath and burst out, "I'm in love with Sahid." My daughter's ability to shift from one subject to another always caught me off guard. I was still reeling from her first admission when she said, "I swear I'll never love anyone as much as I love him. I love him more than Anjuli ever will and Anjuli isn't even nearly as pretty as me."

"Don't be silly," I tried to keep me voice light. "You'll love many men." As soon as the last words came out of my mouth, I knew I had said something terrible. I didn't want her to love any men.

Mythri's upper lip curled into a snarl. "No, that's you, appa. You and mom."

I placed my hands on Mythri's shoulders and shook her lightly. "All I meant is that you will meet more than one man in your life, but yes it's true you very possibly might love only one person." I paused. "You need to know Mythri I did love your mother. I loved her and only her for a long, long time. But things change. You are old enough to understand. No?"

Mythri bit her lip and looked down at the ground. She whispered an apology. I caressed her hair and we started to walk together to the exit. As we did, I noticed Elaine and Sahid in the distance walking together toward the locker rooms.

— ⸙ —

Why do I go on so much about cricket? Because I can't talk about my past life in Sri Lanka, not to my ex-wife, not my friends or teammates, not to Mythri. Where would I start for one thing? Should I say that I had once a loving mother and father, a wonderful childhood with dear friends, thoughtful, caring schoolmasters. Or should I explain that I grew up Tamil and Christian in a country that had, still has, very little tolerance for either? Maybe I should recount the war stories? I can describe the night my life in Sri Lanka ended, the night of the riot.

Or maybe we could skip all that misery and start with one of the happiest times in my life, the year I spent in a refugee camp in India, because it's there where I met two of the finest cricket players I've ever played with and where I really perfected my cricket game. There's a long list of events I can relate to you, and you'll pat my hand kindly and tell me that I'm strong, assure me I'm brave and extraordinary for surviving—as my wife did. Surviving isn't enough.

This is why I need cricket: cricket is my explanation. Cricket allows me to sit in a room of Sri Lankans and talk about something, other than pain and anger. It gives me some way to relate, to no longer be enraged, murderous. Cricket provides extraordinary feats to recount with good humor and good nature—no bitterness, no rancor. My cricket stories will make you laugh, groan, cheer; they won't ever make you weep. Cricket is the link between my childhood, my time in the camp, my university, even fatherhood. You see, for me, every tragic story is a story told in past tense: a recounting of sorrow done never to be undone. Every sports story, on the other hand, is, like all good love stories, a story told in present tense: when the ball twists and arcs and sails and dances, bobs and weaves, there is, in that second, a hundred different happy endings.

Sahid, Elaine, and I met at a café to strategize our next match. Our team had been doing well. We'd lost two matches but then won the next two. If we won our next match, we would qualify for the regionals. The dream was to ultimately play in New York City. But that was some games away.

The team we'd be playing the next day was well known to Sahid and me. They were good. I had attended as many of their games as I could and I'd made a list of their strongest players. I told Sahid I wanted to invite Elaine to the meeting because she was a good strategist, and as our newest player she could bring a fresh eye to things. I was also looking for any reason to spend time with her. I knew by then I was attracted to her, but, because I was the captain, I didn't want to make her feel uncomfortable.

Elaine and Sahid were already seated by the time I had arrived at the café, whispering. I felt a twinge when I saw them like that. They were beautiful together. Two remarkable, intelligent people. They made a gloriously handsome couple.

That impression kept coming to me, unbidden, throughout our meeting, coupled with a helpless sensation, like loss. I had hoped to spend time with Elaine. Now I wondered if I wasn't making a fool of myself. Forty-five minutes into the meeting, I had barely nibbled at my tofu wrap. My coffee had gone cold.

Just then, the front door to the restaurant opened, and my daughter came sashaying through. She sidled up to Sahid, tossed her hair, and batted her eyelashes at him. He stared at her mutely. She pointed to the front window. Five young South Asian teenage girls had lined up along the glass. They were dressed in miniskirts and tight tops, and they were all staring at Sahid. Mythri was explaining that they were all members of the Sahid Chamkanni Fan Club and that they wanted his autograph.

I was about to tell her to leave Sahid alone when he took her hand and walked out with her to the front of the store. The girls jostled and elbowed each other to get to Sahid first.

"I should put a stop to that," I said.

"Why? Sahid will figure out a way to put a stop to it."

"Not against a band of amorous fifteen-year old girls. No one should have to handle that trauma alone." Elaine laughed. I did wonder why Sahid kept allowing himself to be dragged away like that. "Do you think he enjoys it?" I asked Elaine. "The attention?"

"He talks to them because Mythri is *your* daughter." She smiled ruefully. "He loves you you know." I hadn't known that. I wondered how much they had talked about me, and *when* they'd talked about me. "You know. I think this is the first time we've been alone," she said. "You seem to be avoiding me."

"Avoiding no, I just—"

"So let's talk."

This was the opening I'd been waiting for so I started to ask her what she thought about the Indian national team's latest losing streak. She raised her hand, palm forward, and shook her head amiably. "No cricket. I want you to tell me something about yourself." I hesitated. "My choice," she insisted. She seemed to be searching for some safe subject. I knew she wouldn't ask about my ex and my work, and accounting wasn't really a conversation igniter. "Tell me one thing you're really proud of. Something about you—from your past."

I froze, my lips parted, looking for all the world a daft bugger. "I don't know," was all I managed. "There isn't much to me other than cricket." I had meant it only as a joke, but as soon as I said it I knew that it sounded like a rebuff.

I tried to think of something that might salvage the situation but she was staring back out the window, her attention diverted. The girls surrounded Sahid now and they didn't look like they intended to let him go anywhere. "I better go save him," she said.

"I'll go," I offered, though the furiously bopping teenage girls terrified me.

"No, no. Mythri is already miffed at me so there's no harm done when I intervene. Why should we both become unpopular?" So she thought Mythri hated her, which was very possible. No past. Angry daughter. There was no way I was going to win her over now.

"Mythri can be silly at times," I offered. "But she admires you."

Elaine gave a disbelieving smile. "I'll take one for the team," she chirped as she headed for the doorway. I wanted to say something else. I tried to say thank you, but she was already out the door, words trailing like an afterthought. I paid for our coffees and wraps, gathered the diagrams, and headed for the door to try and save my daughter from herself.

The opposing team had put up their best batsmen, but it hadn't mattered. Elaine bowled her finest game of the season. For the first time in the history of the team, we were headed for the regionals. After Elaine bowled, when we knew we had won, Sahid ran up to her, and embraced her. Just before the other teammates hoisted her onto their shoulders regaling her with a round of "She's a Jolly Good Fellow," I saw Sahid whisper something in her ear.

After the game, to my surprise, Mythri ran up and hugged Elaine. She shook Sahid's hand. No fawning. No autographs. A quick, very polite congratulations. She ran up to me and gave me a big hug and kiss on the cheek. I saw her wave at her group of friends, all standing at the boundary watching her. "That was nice. The hug you gave Elaine." Mythri shrugged. I pointed to Mythri's friends. "Sahid's fan club doesn't want to congratulate him?"

"Oh there's no fan club anymore. He's taken," my daughter replied. "He's engaged." My stomach sank. That had been quick, but it made sense. Sahid came from a traditional family. If Elaine and he were committed to a relationship, he would have to show them he was serious about her. Mythri's eyelids fluttered. She brought her hand to her mouth and tittered. "Oops, I wasn't supposed to say something. I was sworn to secrecy." I tried hard to feign indifference. "He was going to tell you tonight," she offered. "At the celebration. Act surprised, okay."

I managed to mimic joy with all the teammates. I promised that I would be at the team celebration that evening, and I would be, even though I had a feeling it was going to be a simultaneously joyful and thoroughly painful and awkward evening. I was slow to get dressed and the last to leave the locker room that night. I was packing my things when Elaine knocked on the locker room door.

"Congratulations," I said. I meant it.

"Yeah, I wasn't sure. When I saw the pitch, I knew you were putting a lot of trust in me—"

"No. Congratulations on your engagement." I feigned gaiety. "I know I'm not supposed to know but Mythri told me about it."

Elaine's eyes widened. "Engagement? What are you talking about?"

"Mythri told me Sahid is engaged."

"Sahid is." She spoke slowly as if explaining something to a child. "His parents have arranged a marriage for him."

"Arranged?" I asked. I felt a bit giddy, and my voice was now pitched an octave higher. "An arranged marriage?" I coughed. "But not with you."

She drew back. "Did you think he was marrying me?" she demanded. "Seriously? I mean we talk. He told me what was happening with his family. He wanted to tell you but I think he was afraid you'd judge him and tell him not to. I think that's why he told Mythri. I think he was hoping she'd tell you first."

I felt my muscles uncoil, the adrenaline rush through me. I released the breath I'd been holding. It was precisely, exactly the sensation I experienced every time I saw the opposing team's wicket disintegrate. I suppressed the desire to pump my fist in the air, to let out a giggle. She scowled. "You're a strange person you know that?"

"And you?" I asked. "You don't judge him?"

She considered this. "I think there are a lot of different paths to love," she replied off-handedly. And even though she hadn't meant it that way—she wasn't thinking of me at all—I felt something right in what she said.

I nodded. "I'm sorry I didn't answer your question the other day," I said to her, an offering of sorts. "But maybe we can go out and get a drink sometime? Talk."

She grew quiet, her expression angry, and for a moment I thought she was going to turn and walk out. Then, something in her relaxed—a recognition. "Are you asking me out?" She smiled slyly.

I took a deep breath. "Yes, but the only thing," I stammered. "It's hard for me to always tell all the things—"

Elaine shook her head. "All you jocks—"

"No," I insisted. "There's more to it than that."

I must have said the last words with more force than I intended because her eyes widened momentarily. Then, she smiled. She reached out and squeezed my arm. "Yes, I'll go for a drink with you, and don't worry so much, Sebastian. As my father used to say, it's only cricket."

We started to walk out of the locker room together. At the door, still not ready to let hope get the best of me, I asked, "What did Sahid whisper to you? Out on the field."

"I don't really know," she replied. "He was speaking in Urdu." She held the locker room door open for me. "But I'm pretty sure he said, 'Thank you, sister. Thank you.'"

The Inter-Continental

⋯ ⚔ ⋯

When Malika's uncle visited Colombo from America, he came by her house to put a chat with us. By then, Malika and I had double pierced our ears, pierced our belly buttons, even our noses. We sported iced-out jewelry around our necks and wrists, and glued painted press-ons to our fingernails. We glossed our crimpy hair with coconut oil and tattooed matching lotuses just at the point where our lower backs sloped into our buttocks.

Despite our parent's disapproval, we plastered posters on our walls of Malinga and Ryan Adams. We listened to 2Pac and Jay-Z, 50 Cent and Bow Wow, Lil' Kim and Eve because they spoke to us about the way we lived. We were nineteen.

Malika's mother hoped her brother, a psychiatrist, could make Malika and me understand we had to start behaving properly. She had started hating on Malika. Maybe there was reason in some of what she said, and I even tried to say so. But then Malika's mum went and claimed Malika's horoscope predicted she would end up dead. This is the kind of nutty talk that ammas love to try but which only makes things worse. At least Uncle didn't speak such nonsense.

We were all in the sitting room, Uncle eying each of us. He was old, over fifty; his hair was graying and the skin along his jaw had loosened,

96

but I could tell he was once very handsome, a little like Iraj. He lingered on Malika's nose ring, his lips twitching. Of all the things we'd done to our bodies—or at least of all the things he knew about—that bothered him the most. It was not something a proper Sinhalese woman did to herself.

"Uncle, would you like another drink?" I asked. I'd always had a small crush on him, ever since I was very young. Malika gave me a tight, annoyed smile.

Her uncle slid his empty tumbler across the coffee table. "Yes, darling. Another scotch." Even though he'd lived in America twenty years, he drew out the word darling as a Sri Lankan would.

When I returned with his drink, he asked us if we were studying hard for our A-levels. He wanted to know how my father was. He reminded me that my father and he had been batchmates at Royal. "Uncle, I've heard all these stories." But he continued speaking. They had many adventures together though Uncle didn't specify. This was his way of letting us know he was very much like Malika and me.

He stopped and peered at us. "What do you plan to do with your lives? You are not children any more." Uncle sipped his scotch. "You should be examples for your nangis and your mallis. You are good girls, no?" When we stared past him, he raised a thinning eyebrow. He knew what it meant to be afraid, he told us. He knew what it was like to believe there was no future.

He said this as if he meant it. But he couldn't possibly. He remembered this country as it was before the war started. To him, it was once a good place to live. The soldiers on the streets surprised him; the checkpoints confounded him. He refused to see the corruption. He spoke of the government as if it deserved respect. But we of course knew better.

"You have futures," he insisted. "You could accomplish great things for Sri Lanka. Bring peace even." We nodded so he would think he was reaching us.

The next time Uncle visited, it was late December. He brought with him his youngest daughter, Kishani. She was two years younger than us, and I could tell very different. She was sweet, for one thing. *Hari lassana*, Malika's mother made a point of saying, staring at Malika as she said it.

Kishani sat, her long skirt billowing around her ankles. And, despite the heat, she wore a blouse with wide sleeves that covered her elbows. I wondered if she thought she was visiting a Buddhist temple, instead of a Colombo home. Malika must have noticed too, because she made a comment about liking Kishani's blouse. Malika said this with a sneer, and I felt a little sorry, so I said I liked it too. Kishani smiled and politely thanked us both.

When Malika sat down, her shorts rode up and exposed the pale, yellow flesh of her upper thighs. When she turned in her seat, the waist-band pulled down to reveal part of her tattoo. Kishani started when she noticed it.

Even I thought Malika's shorts and skirts too revealing. When she walked along the street, men stared, called things to her, tried to touch and to pinch. These men always scared me a little. But Malika was tall and strong and had a bad temper. She'd shout *Ballige putha!* if some-one came too close. I knew no other girl who cursed like her. I had seen Malika's fury make grown men cower.

That's what had always drawn me to her. Malika always did things her own way. She shortened the hems of her school uniform and left the top buttons of her blouse undone. To her cousin's wedding, she wore a sari only, no jacket underneath. She openly mocked the aunties and uncles and called them hypocrites—which they were though nobody else dared tell them so. And she didn't care about punishment. I cared, though I always tried to hide this. But she wasn't a coward like me.

After Kishani finished her passion fruit cordial, Malika asked if she'd like to watch DVDs in her room. Kishani nodded. Malika sig-naled to me to follow.

Malika's room was still caught somewhere between a child's and a grownup's. On one wall, Hello Kitty stickers circled a poster of a smil-ing terrier puppy. The top shelves of the only bookcase displayed all her swimming and tennis trophies even though she'd given up competing long ago; piled on the bottom shelves were textbooks from the business courses she was following at university. On another wall she'd taped posters of Sanga—who I didn't find attractive, myself, because he was married and old but who Kishani claimed to want even more because he was both—of Gwen Stefani and Justin Timberlake. Strewn on her bed and crammed in her closet were clothes—leopard prints, sequin, lace—all very short and cut low.

Malika swept the clothes from the bed and made room for Kishani to sit. She slipped a DVD into her laptop and stretched out beside her cousin.

The machine whirred and sputtered; the DVD began mid-scene. An Indian woman wearing only a thong slathered oil on her body. I stared mesmerized more by the image's unexpectedness than by what the woman was doing. The woman tilted forward at the waist, took the bottle of oil and slipped it up and down between her heavy breasts. She moaned as she did this, loud. I ran to the laptop and turned the sound down. What would Malika's parents or Uncle think if they heard?

Kishani watched, her eyes narrowed. I couldn't tell if she was shocked or amused. But it was Malika who surprised me. She wasn't watching the DVD. Instead, she was lying on the bed carefully scrutinizing her cousin's face.

"Indian porn is not as good as American," said Malika. "The Americans have much better bodies, no?" Her voice was low and syrupy. Malika was the kind of person who had to prod and poke at anything lovely, as if such things were an insult against her.

"I think it's foul," Kishani replied. Her eyelids fluttered and her voice caught momentarily. "I don't really get it. The people look silly. Like that." Kishani gestured at the screen. The woman straddled a man; her breasts and head bounced wildly from side to side as the man held her waist and moved her up and down over his groin. "Who's turned on by something like that?"

"Obviously, Malika is," I replied. I tried to smile, but the truth was I was angry. I had started, recently, to dislike Malika's need to provoke just because she could. I had begun to hate the pointlessness of her actions.

Malika flushed; her lips tightened. She slid from the bed and flounced out of the room. I stopped the DVD. Kishani and I followed.

Uncle stood at the front door, readying to leave; he told Kishani to gather her things. Malika took his arm, leaned into him, and tilted her head coyly. "John-mama, Kishani should spend New Year's Eve with me and my friends. At the Inter-Continental." Uncle's eyes widened a little, but Kishani jumped gleefully.

"I'd really like that. That would be fun," she said. Uncle sputtered.

Malika must have guessed that Uncle was searching for a polite reason to say no because she grabbed me by the arm and thrust me forward. "Samantha will be there. She'll make sure Kishani is safe, mama." Uncle smiled kindly at me, and my stomach dropped.

Kishani, who up to that point had been pleading with her father, stopped short. Her face fell. "I didn't bring anything nice to wear."

"You could wear one of my saris," Malika's mum suggested.

Malika groaned. "She'll look ancient. Only old people wear saris on New Year's"

"I'll take you to ODEL, Kishani," I offered, my desire to please Uncle getting the better of me. Kishani clutched her hands in front of her chest and bounced on her toes. She begged her father.

Uncle glanced at me, took a deep breath, and nodded.

"They renamed it the Ceylon Continental, but we still call it by the old name." Kishani stared up at the Inter-Continental, tall and white against the glassine sky. On our way to ODEL, I'd driven her by the hotel to show her where we would spend New Year's Eve. The Inter-Continental stood at the end of Galle Face Green, next to the old Parliament building and the army barracks. The beach stretched out in front of it. Kishani had wanted to walk in the sand, so I parked to the side.

It was late morning and already very warm. Seagulls dived at squealing children. Siri siri bags, caught by the wind, tumbled and fluttered across the sand. Tourists, broad-brimmed hats flapping in their faces, trained their cameras at the ocean. The sea was calm, and bathers had waded in, some to their waists others to their chests. Occasionally, in the distance, the heads of swimmers bobbed above the waves. Vendors lined the sidewalk: one hawked Elephant Castle ice cream, the other boiled chickpeas, another, at the far end, displayed kites in all colors, sizes, and shapes—butterflies, lanterns, Rok kites decorated with images of cartoon superheroes, and multicolored kytoons.

I explained to Kishani that this area was called the Fort because the Dutch and English used it to defend the city. I pointed to the old cannons, impotent looking now. I showed her the Watchtower, once a lighthouse. I named the statues in front of the Old Parliament Building: all former prime ministers. I gestured to the end of the beach, past a line of king coconut palms, fronded heads bent and lolling in the warm breeze, to a smaller, ancient-looking building. "That is the Galle Face Hotel. Your amma and thaththa were married there."

"It's all so lovely," Kishani whispered.

We removed our shoes and walked to the water. A wave rushed toward us and washed over our feet: the sweet warmth of it pleasurable compared to the burning sun on our necks. Strips of seaweed and crushed seashells, the ocean's fingerprint, remained after the water receded. I nudged a broken conch with my toe.

The breeze caught Kishani's hair, sending dark tendrils whipping about her face. I reached over and brushed the strands from her eyes. "It's hard to believe there's a war going on," she said.

"There's an army barracks. Just behind that wall." I pointed to a long stone fortification tufted with barbed wire. "There are soldiers with guns trained on you and me. On everyone here. In case." Kishani shielded her eyes with her hand and surveyed the wall.

"I don't see anyone."

"You're not supposed to."

"My father talks about coming back here, after he retires."

"If you have a lot of money and a foreign passport, this is not a bad

place to live," I said. "But I want to get away. I'll go to Australia soon."
I had never told anyone this before. I didn't dare. My parents would
be crushed—I'm their only child. Malika would laugh at me; she'd
say I wasn't the kind of person who did such things. "When I'm rich,
I'll make a decision whether to come back or not." It wasn't my voice
speaking. This voice was strong and firm. But Kishani wasn't someone
who could judge me—like Malika—or even know how impossible it
was to leave now. For her, it was plausible, what I said.

"It's so bad here?" Kishani asked.

I pointed to a row of pro-military posters. "The government talks
peace but it's all rubbish." How to explain the feeling that you are swimming underwater? You can see where the light hits the surface but, as
hard as you try, you can never reach it. "They're in it only for themselves.
It's fucked up."

"It's the same in the States," Kishani offered.

"Anyone who is honest is killed." No matter how you protect yourself
they come in the night. Crawl over the walls. Ply the catcher with arrack
so that he will be too drunk to call a warning. They shoot you in the face
when you open the door. Or, else they bribe your neighbor. They wait for
you on the rooftop next door and shoot you as you get into your car. You
cannot be a good person in this country and survive.

Kishani's expression sobered, and, for a moment, I hated her. Why
did she care? She feigned shock this bloody country was blowing up,
but next week she'd fly back to the States where she'd be safe. I grabbed
her by the shoulder and pushed her, maybe a little roughly, toward the
car. We should go to ODEL, I told her, before it became too crowded.

In the car, Kishani pointed to a mini-dress, lying on the back seat,
still wrapped in plastic from the cleaners. It was covered in silver sequin;
I'd saved a long time for such an outfit. "This is what you're wearing for
New Year's?"

I nodded. "It's my favorite. It sparkles in the light."

"Like you," Kishani said. Her face beamed with friendship and
confidence. "It's beautiful and sparkling just like you." I felt my throat
tighten and for a moment tears came to my eyes.

No, I wanted to tell her. Nothing at all like me.

Malika's boyfriend, Shahid, had reserved a suite on the top floor of the Inter-Continental. Shahid's father was very rich—the vice president of a bank—and that made Shahid a bit of a mad bugger. Careless with everything: his money, his possessions, his mates. But he was easy enough to manage if you were used to him.

A group of us readied ourselves in the bedroom. We would dress, get pissed, and then go to a few of the Colombo parties. We'd return later that evening and get pissed some more. The same thing we always did, every night. The one difference: we had a posh room to trash.

Malika stood in front of the mirror, wrapped in a towel, a margarita in one hand. I had already dressed and sat to the side. I hated primping.

Kishani had also dressed. She had bought a red chiffon frock from ODEL, and every time she moved the fabric outlined the curves of her slim body. Shahid and one of his friends, Kumar, sat on the bed, swigging beer. They watched as she applied eyeliner. Shahid leaned toward her, "You are one fine girl," he said.

"Like Beyoncé," chortled Kumar.

Kishani flipped her hair coyly at the two boys. Malika rolled her eyes.

"I have a gift for the American," declared Shahid. He pulled out a clear plastic packet of coke. He dangled it in front of Kishani. "You like?"

Kishani hesitated I stood and grabbed at the packet. "Are you daft? What if we get caught?"

But Shahid was too quick; he held it out of my reach. "Kishani is a big girl," he declared. "She knows what she's doing." Kumar looked on, amused.

"Yeah, Sam." Malika smirked. "This is her party too."

"You don't need to do this," I urged Kishani, but Shahid had already taken her arm and was leading her over to a small table.

"Leave her alone," I persisted. The drugs didn't bother me. I just didn't see why Shahid had to involve Kishani in his insanity. "She isn't like us."

Shahid stopped. "Are we so horrible?" he asked Kishani. Kishani shook her head but didn't look at me. Shahid winked. "So when exactly are you becoming a bhikkhuni, Sam?" Malika giggled.

"Stop them," I hissed to Malika.

Her eyes grew wide, mock-innocent. "Why go agro on *me*? I'm not forcing her."

"I've done this before, Sam," Kishani said over her shoulder.

I didn't believe her. But she was in the soup now. If she wanted to let those jokers bully her who was I to meddle? That's what Sri Lanka teaches you: don't give a damn about anything or anybody.

I grabbed my handbag and my makeup. I wasn't going to wait in the suite and watch what happened next. "Where are you going," Malika called mockingly after me as I left. "To get ready in the lobby washroom?"

I stood in the hallway, breathing hard. Malika was right. I had nowhere to go.

I heard the door to the suite click behind me. I turned, hoping it was Kishani. She'd changed her mind. But it was Kumar. "I have my room if you want to come with me," he said. "Calm down a little." His expression was kind, like he understood and believed I was right. He grabbed my wrist and led me down the hall.

Once inside, he sat on the edge of the bed and patted the empty space beside him. "Come on, Samantha. I'll help you relax. I'll give you a massage." Predictable. Why had I expected more out of any of them?

I walked to far end of the room. As I stood there, I imagined Malika and Shahid, maybe even Kishani, blackguarding me in the other room. My face burned with the thought and, at that moment, what I wanted most was to get some air and cool my skin. The room had a large, sectioned window that spanned the far wall; it looked out at Galle Face Green and the ocean beyond. Street lamps and New Year's decorations lit the Green. Headlights left trails of luminescence along

Galle Road. Beyond the beach, the ocean gleamed obsidian. I tried to open one of the windows. It was easy enough to jimmy the cheap lock with my fingernail. The warm air hit me immediately, so much more soothing than the false chill of the air-conditioned room.

In front of me was a cement ledge about three feet wide. I stared at it first. But suddenly it felt as if I needed to be out there. Mental I know, but I just wanted to test myself, to see if I could control my body. I wanted to act in a way not even Malika would have the nerve to.

I threw off my heels, crawled up onto the windowsill, and placed a foot on the ledge. Behind me, Kumar jumped up from the bed. Keeping my back pressed hard against the glass, I slowly slid my body up, until I was standing. I edged myself over, so that Kumar could not reach me easily.

The wind rushed at me and through me. My hair loosened and lashed, painfully, at my cheeks and forehead. My dress fluttered against my body. Strands of hair caught in my eyes and mouth.

Colombo stretched out before me. I could see the lights of the World Trade Center, still on, though all the employees left long ago. Below me, people teemed the streets. Cheap firecrackers sputtered and faded, like ash dropped from the butt of a cigarette. I heard nothing but the rush of the wind and the ocean beyond it. The air smelled, not of exhaust as I had expected, but salty and sweet.

It beggars all belief, I know, but I wasn't scared. All I had to do was concentrate on the view: the old colonial porticos of the Galle Face Hotel lit up for New Year's Eve; the advertisements on the billboard, one for Omega watches, the other for a cell phone company; the army barracks, its watchtowers silhouetted against the city lights. It was all much smaller; I was a giant, looming over it.

"What the fuck are you doing?" Kumar called to me. I yelled over the wind, "Join me."

Kumar tried to place a foot on the ledge. He fell back into the room as if pushed. A few minutes later, he stuck his head out the window. "Come." He held out his arm, a parent calling an errant child. "Let's go back to Malika. I'll help you."

But I wasn't afraid. I didn't need his help.

I don't know how long I was out there. Fifteen minutes. Perhaps twenty. After a while I wasn't even looking at the scene before me. I just allowed myself to step over the dark sea, into the night, into the stars. I had never felt like this. I was brave. Powerful. All the things I'd never been.

In the distance, over the rush of the wind, I heard a quick rapping. A few seconds, the sound repeated, this time more urgent. Kumar withdrew for a moment, and then called to me. "Samantha. It's the manager. He's at the door and wants to come in. I have to let him in." He had his hands on the ledge. Half of his body was out the window. "Please. You don't know what they'll do to us, if they see you like this." I turned my head slowly and edged toward him. When I crouched so that I could get my body through the open window, I lost my balance and pitched forward. The street below surged up at me, and I felt sure I would fall. Not that I minded. But Kumar grabbed me by the waist and pulled me into the room. My head hit the window frame with a crack. We rolled onto the carpet.

The knocking became banging; the room door flung open. Two soldiers barreled in. They both gripped automatic rifles. Behind them followed a hotel manager.

One of the soldiers prodded Kumar with his boot. "Get up," he demanded. Kumar stood, his hands up in front of him. I slid backward and pressed my back against the bed. "You also." The soldier motioned with his gun. I stood slowly. My head ached furiously when I did, and I teetered slightly.

"You've been drinking," the soldier observed. I shook my head. The pain was awful.

The manager stepped in front of the soldiers. "Sir, sir, very sorry to bother you," he said to Kumar. "But there have been reports on the street. Someone taking pictures of the army base. From this room." A soldier grabbed Kumar's kit and upended it onto the bed; a t-shirt and jeans, a bottle of cologne, a packet of condoms tumbled out. The soldier scowled.

"I don't even have a camera," protested Kumar. The other soldier grabbed my handbag and emptied it onto the floor. He studied the contents as if he'd discovered something incriminating. Finally, he placed his boot over a compact and slowly crushed it. Kumar and the manager gaped.

"It was me," I admitted. "I was on the window ledge." Everyone stared at me, then at the open window. "You saw my dress in the light. It sparkles. My dress twinkles." The soldiers looked me up and down incredulously as if they had stumbled on an alien life form.

The manager threw up his hands. "But madam, those windows shouldn't be opened."

"I wanted to see the city. Up close."

The soldier who had crushed my compact case took a step toward me. "Show me your identity card." My gaze didn't waver. Despite my aching skull, I didn't flinch. I knew better.

The manager held his hands before him, as if carrying an especially cumbersome serving tray. "Sir, this gentleman," he pointed to Kumar, "is Ananda Perera's son. He is a patriot."

"He still must show me his ID if I ask for it."

But the other soldier, the one sorting through Kumar's things, gave an exasperated snort. "They are wasting our time." He pointed at me but spoke to the manager. "I can have this one arrested. She will spend New Year's Eve at the police station." He glanced sideways at me. "Not a nice place for a pretty girl." When I didn't acknowledge him, he grimaced. "She's lucky I don't have time to waste on people like her." He jabbed the manager's shoulder. "We will leave now. But we hear any more reports of high jinks," he glared at me, "we will return and search the luggage of every guest." The manager closed his eyes.

After the soldiers had left, Kumar collapsed onto the bed, head in hands. The manager still hadn't moved. "My father will make some calls tomorrow," Kumar muttered. "He will put everything right."

The manager's mouth worked but no sound came. Finally, he gazed at me, forlornly. The whites of his eyes were jaundiced; the corneas tinged blue. "Madam, no more going out the window," he begged.

Kumar and I didn't move for minutes. He sat, hunched over, breathing as if he'd sprinted miles. I closed the window and gathered my wallet and car keys. I tried to clean the remains of the compact, nothing more than shards of glass and plastic and rouge ground into the carpet. Kumar didn't acknowledge me.

I left him and ran down the hall to the suite. Malika was still at the mirror, applying makeup. Kishani sprawled face down on the bed. I was about to demand what else Shahid had given her when Kishani sprang up. "Hey there, gorgeous," she chirped before falling back.

"What the hell happened to you, men," Malika exclaimed when she saw me. "Your hair is ruined. What are you going to do now?"

I ignored her. I grabbed Kishani by the shoulder and helped her stand. Before Kishani could protest, I put an arm around her shoulders and maneuvered her to the door. Malika and Shahid were too immobilized by shock to stop me.

I guided Kishani down the hall. She kept asking me where I was taking her, but I gripped her tightly. I pushed her into the lift.

Kishani and I stumbled together through the hotel lobby. Around me tourists in evening gowns and tuxedos milled asking directions to various clubs and hotspots; locals in saris tried to assist them. The manager, the one who had come to Kumar's room earlier, frowned. He made a move as if to stop me, but then thought better of it.

Outside, in the parking lot, Kishani broke free. "Where are you taking me?"

"Home." A spasm of pain shot down my skull and neck. I winced and brought a hand to my head.

Kishani took a step toward me. "Are you all right?" I waved her away.

She looked back at the entrance to the hotel, and I thought for a minute, she was going to go back inside to Malika and Shahid. I experienced a flash of terror, unlike anything I'd felt on the ledge, and I had to keep from gripping her arm. I'd broken with my friends. I couldn't go back and if she left me I'd be alone. But she only sighed. "It's hard, pretending all the time." She wrapped her arms around her as if she were cold. "Let's go."

I took her to my car and helped her into the passenger seat. I sat at the steering wheel, my head throbbing. "Can you drive?" Kishani asked.

"Well, you're in no condition to."

She considered for a moment. "The truth is I don't feel anything," she said. "I mean I have an awful taste in my mouth. Like Robitussin gone bad. But I don't think the cocaine is having an effect on me."

I was about to explain it never did the first time. That was the trick of it. At that moment, she probably believed she was immune. Perhaps she even felt proud because of this. But the next morning she would awake, stare up at the ceiling, and experience not physical pain, but a sorrow that would make her muscles and bones ache. She would understand in that moment what a gift she had had: to feel nothing. But I didn't tell her. I didn't have the right. She'd find out soon enough on her own.

"That's good," I said, instead. I reached over and squeezed her hand. She shivered at my touch. I could sense, in the half-light of the parking lot, a change: the downward turn of her mouth, the droop of shoulders. Disappointment or fatigue or both. "Please don't worry," I begged. "Tonight, I'll look after you. I promise."

Ismail

ow to explain why my brother Harry and I stood in my best
friend Abdul's backyard at two in the morning carrying five
large mason jars filled with milk and turkey parts we'd bought at Fair-
way? My brother was supposed to be watching me closely, waiting for
my cue. Instead he was staring at the neighbor's house, terrified. "I
think I saw a light," he whispered.

I don't know why he was so afraid. Abdul, his sister Ameena, and
their parents had returned to Guyana for all of August. No one was in
the house or in the little cottage in the back where Abdul lived. Sure,
the neighbors were Ukrainians with bad, bad tempers, and, true, they
owned guns. But it was three in the morning, and they had long ago
gone to bed.

Harry was thin with dark skin, and I could barely see him in the
night. I was trying to signal to him to stay calm, but he was so busy
gaping at the Ukrainians' house he didn't see the headlights approaching. I pushed my brother behind some bushes as a patrol car crept by.
Its headlights sparked the drizzle creating two shimmering halos. After
the cops had passed, I realized I'd stopped breathing. I gulped as if
surfacing from a long dive.

Between the two of us, we carried five jars. Harry carried a Duane

Reade shopping bag filled with three; my shopping bag held two. We were going to place the jars among Abdul's things, a sort of prank. In the August heat, with no one home to find the jars, the turkey and milk would rot, causing a chemical reaction. Gas would build up inside the jar. If all went as planned, the gas would eventually build up until the jars exploded, covering everything Abdul owned with rotting turkey, spoiled milk, and shards of glass. In other words, we were carrying our own homemade versions of stink bombs.

But Harry, I could tell, was having reservations. Harry put his bag down and turned as if he was about to do a hundred yard sprint. I grabbed him and shook him, hard. He deflated when I did that. He sighed and picked up his bag.

We crept past the main house, into the backyard, toward Abdul's cottage. I whispered to Harry. "Give me the keys."

My brother didn't move. I repeated my request.

"Ameena's going to leave me over this." Did I mention that Abdul's sister Ameena was Harry's girlfriend? That's important.

"You told me you guys are over."

"But I don't want to hurt her, Ismail," he whined.

"Think of this as a surprise. We'll all be sitting in Burger King a month from now laughing."

"Are you kidding, anna? You think Abdul is going to chuckle when he comes home and finds rotting turkey meat exploded all over his stuff."

My brother had a point, but I was determined. Water had seeped through my Nike Air Max. My ankles itched. I looked down and realized I was sinking slowly into a bed of soggy pine needles. This was not the time to have this conversation. "Thevadiya paiya!" I spat. "Go and fuckin' leave me out here alone to do your dirty work. Like you always do. Like you did to akka." Harry stepped back, shocked.

I realize now how pathetic I sounded, but the crazy part is Harry didn't leave. Instead, he stared at me like I'd slapped him in the face. He took the keys out of his pocket and opened the door himself.

At one point, Abdul's cottage sheltered gardening tools and a riding lawn mower. The cottage had also served, for about six months, as

a painting studio when Abdul's mother had taken a landscape painting class at the Art Students League.

In its latest incarnation, as Abdul's home away from home, it
housed a futon, a broken dresser, a stack of DVDs—porn and early Jet
Li films—a television and DVD player, two posters of Gwen Stefani, a
Freddy vs. Jason poster, a window air-conditioning unit, and a worktable with a computer. The place reeked, a potent combination of
unwashed t-shirts, old sneakers, and the ammonia stench of liquid fer-
tilizer. How Abdul could stand sleeping in there, I never understood.

We waited for our eyes to adjust. A syrupy, gray light, oozed around
sheets of paper taped to the windows. I could just make out the rim of
my brother's Yankees cap and the ends of his knotted do-rag. Harry
gripped his stomach, doubled over, and moaned. "C'mon stop fucking with me," I whispered to him.

He looked up at me with an expression of pain so keen that, for a
second, my insides flipped. But I caught myself. We had to focus. We
had to be strategic about where we placed jars.

I put down my bag and removed a sheet of paper from a window-
pane so we'd have light to work by. Harry protested.

"Nobody'll see," I whispered.

"How do you know? We shouldn't take a chance."

"Don't worry so much." I mocked him, using a whiny, baby voice.
"You'll get another tummy ache." Even as I spoke, I knew I'd gone too
far. Maybe I was still mad about the scene outside the cottage. His face
twisted into a tight, hard knot: real hate. But then suddenly he relaxed
and his face took the sweet expression of acceptance, like one of those
saints on those candles they sell in the bodegas.

"Let's do this and get out of here," he said. I nodded an affirmative.

Harry started to place a jar in the middle of the room. "Not there!"
I hissed.

I carefully slid across the floor, holding my hands out so that I could
feel my way and immediately bumped into something. It fell to the
floor with the force of a nuclear explosion. We held our breath until the
distant barking of dogs replaced the clatter. I emptied the clothes in

the dresser drawers onto the floor. Then I took the posters down. "No need to damage Gwen," I whispered. I folded each poster with care and then placed two jars near the cot and a jar next to the DVD player. I spread a thin layer of caulk along the rim of each jar lid, to seal it. I rose and pointed to the worktable. "Put two over there."

When Harry tried to pick up a jar, it slipped in his hands, and he almost dropped it. He looked over at me like he was afraid I was going to start yelling at him. I pretended I hadn't noticed.

Harry put the jar where I asked and then begged to go.

But I had one more thing to do before I left. I walked over to the worktable and untacked a photograph from Abdul's wall. I held it to the window and studied it in the half-light. I could see that it was a photograph of Abdul, some girls, and me, hamming it up at a nightclub. I tore it into pieces. "Why'd you do that?" Harry whispered hoarsely. "He'll know it's us who broke in." I tore up another photograph, one that didn't include me, and then another. When I was finished, all that remained was carnage: a pile of eyes and ears, a slice of arm, a disembodied smile. Harry stared at me his face half anger, half something else, a look of recognition and despair, the same look the driver gives just as he loses control, just before his car makes impact.

—————

Harry and I come from a town near Matara, Sri Lanka. We moved with my dad to Jamaica, Queens, in 1999 when I was fifteen and my brother was eight. My dad is Muslim and my mom is Tamil. In Sri Lanka, the civil war had already been going three years when I was born, and by 1999, when I left, things were still really bad. We didn't get much news from the papers: government censorship. But even as a kid, I understood what was happening. The JVP had moved up north and were killing the LTTE. The LTTE tried to assassinate the leader of the SLFP. The UNP ordered the closing of the universities to crush the JVP. The war created a whole new sick little alphabet. A rearranging of letters was all it took to bring a new wave of violence.

My dad won the visa lottery, but they gave us only three visas. Harry and I have a sister, but she stayed behind. My mom chose Harry, even though he was the youngest, saying that as a boy he would have more opportunity in America. We left promising we would arrange for my mom and my sister to join us as soon as we could. Then 9/11 happened. No more visas. A year later my sister left to take a job as a maid for a family in Kuwait.

Harry couldn't forgive himself for being chosen. It wasn't even like he begged to go. But he felt responsible. And when our sister left for Kuwait he cried for days. We'd all heard the stories. We knew what happened to the Sri Lankan girls who went alone overseas. Harry and I made a pact to stay close, to protect each other. Back then, before Ameena and Abdul, family was all we had.

Harry wasn't just the more sensitive brother; he was also the smarter one. I nearly flunked tenth grade; Harry took AP and honors classes. Still, I did well enough my first year at Queens Community College to transfer to John Jay. I dreamt of becoming a cop or even a forensic scientist like the ones you see on the Discovery channel. But when my dad needed someone in the family to earn a little extra money he asked me to drop out of college and get a full-time job. My dad, a taxi driver, couldn't make enough money to send for my mother. So at nineteen, I dropped out of school and took a job as a line cook at the local Kabab Kaiser. That's how I met Abdul.

Abdul's dad owned a chain of Kabab Kaisers and when Abdul finished high school gave him a job as manager of the flagship restaurant, the one where I got my job. Even though Abdul was my boss, we became friends immediately. Abdul said work was work and when we played we were equals. Of course, even at play he had way more money than I did, but that didn't stop us from becoming close.

We mostly talked, and drank, and smoked dope, and sometimes did a line or two. About a month into our relationship we got the idea of making the turkey bombs. My tenth grade chem teacher had told the class about them; he'd described being a teenager and spending months perfecting the recipe. The idea kind of caught hold of me, and, at that time, whatever caught hold of me caught hold of Abdul also.

We used one of the abandoned buildings you find along the MetroNorth tracks on Sutphin Boulevard. First, we started with buckets—the kind house paint comes in—but we didn't have much luck. Then Abdul found a website that suggested using mason jars—for a more dramatic effect. That worked but only occasionally. And then we just got tired of it—I mean, seriously, how long can you get your kicks from exploded turkeys?—and we moved on.

Mostly I just wanted a reason to spend time with Abdul. Until I met Abdul, I hadn't realized how lonely I was. I had my brother and my father, and I had one or two friends in school, but it was hard having to work and study. Abdul and I clicked in a way I hadn't with anyone else in America. We were so close Abdul even introduced Ameena to my brother. "We're keepin' it in the family," he joked.

If you go long enough without something, sex, money, even love, you can get to the point you don't need it. But if you suddenly have access to what's missing, get it back into your life, then you'll do whatever it takes to keep that thing. The thought of loss knocks you flat on the floor, your chest caved in, gasping for air.

For a time, that's what knowing Abdul felt like. I'd been okay without him, but once we were friends, I couldn't imagine what it would be like to lose him. There were days that thought alone—the thought of that loss—left me knocked out on the floor, chest caved in, gasping for air.

⁕

When my brother and I finally got home from Abdul's house, I went to my bedroom—a corner of our sitting room with a sheet tacked up so that I could have a little privacy—and crashed. My sleep was disturbed an hour later by my dad performing fajr. My dad wasn't very religious. Between his jobs, trying to make rent, and saving enough to buy his own taxi medallion—something he would never be able to do though he kept on trying—he didn't have the time. But something would always happen to remind him, and he'd start up again, for a little while.

I was exhausted, so my dad's prayers didn't wake me. They wove their way into my sleep, and I started to dream of Sri Lanka, of a city called Batticaloa turned battleground during the war. My brother and I were visiting an uncle there. When we got of the train, we saw immediately men on bikes, machine guns slung over their shoulders. In the middle of the town's mosque was a crater where a bomb had gone off. We put our prayer mats right around the hole. The sun came through the broken roof and burned through my shirt as I knelt.

Everyone prayed as if a hole in the middle of a mosque was nothing extraordinary. But I stared. The crater was dark and deep and pieces of the clay and wood, which once had made up the dome, stuck out from the dirt. These pieces—bleached by the sun and rain—didn't look so much like parts of a building as they did bones. I imagined, scared myself, thinking these were the bones of those killed by the bomb, though I knew the bodies had been removed long before. In my dreams—because I dreamt of this mosque often—those pieces always turned into bones, the bones of my parents, the bones of Harry and my sister, of Abdul, of me.

Every time I had this nightmare, I woke up drenched in sweat, my pajamas and futon soaked. I lay in bed for a couple of hours just trying to breathe.

By the time I dressed and lifted back the sheet, my dad had finished praying and was outside cleaning the taxi he leased. Our neighbor stood on the doorstep smoking a cigarette. Her head was covered by a fuchsia dupatta; even in the heat, she wore a long-sleeved shirt and jeans. She gave me a sideways glance when I strutted out of the house. "What up, son?" I called to her as I passed.

She blew a stream of smoke in my direction. "Your faux-ghetto pose don't work on me, Ismail. You're right off the boat. Just like I am."

From his room, Harry was blasting 8ball and MJG, loud. He was trying to drown out his memories of the night before. I was about to go ask my dad if he needed help, when I heard the sound of the window sash being slid open. The blast of music caused my neighbor to step backwards as if pushed. She shook her head furiously, flicked her cigarette stub in our flowerbed, and stomped off to her apartment. My brother motioned for me to come inside. I crawled through his window.

My brother was sitting on the edge of his bed with his head in his hands. Harry had always been thin, but lately he'd grown gaunt, his face pinched. Too much studying he claimed every time I asked. "We have to go back," my brother said as I sat down. "We have to clean up before Ameena comes home."

"It's just a joke, yo. Abdul will figure out some way to retaliate and then everything will be alright."

"But Ameena will hate me." My brother grimaced and grabbed his stomach.

"What do you care what that bitch thinks of you? You guys are over."

"We're not over," my brother gasped. "Not completely. I asked her to marry me." He was breathing hard. His face twisted with every word. "I was rushing her and she became afraid."

I shook my head. "You are one pissu mother-fucker."

"I think there may be a chance."

This was my brother: always second-guessing. He couldn't commit to anything. "This was your idea too. I mean, thambi, if there was a chance, then why'd you agree?"

My brother hunched forward. "You do a lot for us. You're working so that I can go to school." His voice was growing strained, and I wanted to go to him. But I also needed to play it cool. He bit his lip. "But this shit's all fucked up man. I can't think straight."

I shrugged. I was tired of this conversation. I was tired of my brother, of Abdul, of everyone. I pointed at him. "Hey, there are two morons, a big one and a little one, sitting on a stump in the woods."

Harry shook his head and ignored me. "I guess I agreed because I was mad at Ameena," Harry persisted. "I was mad at her after the fight."

"One moron falls off the stump. Which one?"

"We got to go back, anna." My brother doubled over and started to cough.

I stood up. "The big one. The big one fell off."

Harry grimaced. "Please," he begged. "Please."

He was a little peaked, now. It was enough to make me almost want to try and fix things. But I couldn't. " 'Cause the other one," I said. "He was a little moron," My brother let out a long groan.

"Get it. A little MORE-on." I forced a chuckle. "You got to admit. It's kind of funny—"

But Harry didn't hear me because seconds later he collapsed on the floor. When I ran to him, he was curled up, a puddle of bloody vomit and drool forming on the carpet beside him. I ran out of the room, screaming for my father.

— ◆ —

Ameena wasn't the prettiest desi girl I knew. She had a long, angular face and she was as skinny and dark as Harry. Even her own brother thought she was plain; that's why he had wanted to fix her up with my brother. Geek love, he'd called it.

And they did fall in love. Overnight. Harry started spending all his free time with her. It got to the point that my father had to remind him to study, to keep his grades up. Harry listened to my dad—he was always dutiful that way—but he didn't stop seeing Ameena.

He and Ameena liked most to hang out at the Burger King on Jamaica Avenue. They ruled the joint. Apart there wasn't anything special about either of them; together they became—how else to put it?—powerful. Harry suddenly became super popular, even the stupid, pretty Bratz doll girls flirted with him. One day, we were hanging out with one of Abdul's friends—someone who hadn't realized yet Abdul had a sister. He pointed to Ameena and said, "Machans, that shorty over there, she looks mad potente. No?" Abdul and I both nearly fell out of our seats when we heard him say this. Ameena pretty? Could being in love really make you change like that? Could it really make you beautiful when, before, you weren't?

I was jealous of them. I admit that. It shocked me how love made

Harry forget about all we, my father and me, were doing for him. It shocked me that he stopped worrying about my sister—or at least seemed distracted when I mentioned her. It was like, in all his happiness, there was no room for our unhappiness. Love doesn't just make you more beautiful, I guess. Love also makes you lose all sympathy for those of us who don't have your luck.

⸺ ⚜ ⸺

As the paramedics carried him out on the stretcher Harry was on his cell phone with his friends begging one of them to call Ameena in Guyana and tell her he was being taken to the hospital. My father and I followed the ambulance in his taxi.

The emergency room was crammed: elderly people slumped over and drooling onto their laps; tykes throwing up on the hospital floor as their parents cradled their heads; two distraught black men, blood covering their shirts, screaming in French; and hordes of people with nothing visibly wrong with them. After the paramedics spoke with the nurse, an orderly rolled my brother into a hospital corridor, and placed him in a line of stretchers.

My father stood over Harry, holding his hand and stroking the hair from his face. I stood to the side folding the pile of Harry's clothes the nurses had handed me. Harry moaned pitifully.

As I shook them out, Harry's jeans rang, a chirring that caused a volley of groans down the line of stretchers. "Ismail," Harry moaned, "get that. It could be Ameena."

The last thing I wanted to do was talk to Harry's ex-girlfriend, but I fished through the pockets and found the cell. I flipped it open. "Sup, yo."

There was a long silence on the other end. I was about to hang up when a guy's trembling voice asked, "Harry's not dead, is he?"

"Fuck no, asshole. What you want?"

There was a sigh of relief. "Tell him Ameena's going to try and call him tomorrow."

I flipped the cell phone shut. "Was it Ameena?" Harry asked.

"No," I replied. I almost didn't tell him Ameena was planning to call. I almost let it go. But then he groaned, long and loud. "She's going to call," I said. "Tomorrow." A look of joy—better than any medicine a doctor could have given him—passed across his face.

Truth be known, I didn't like Harry hanging out with Ameena. I guess you could say I was jealous. Before Ameena, Harry came to me with his problems; he was always asking my advice. But after he met Ameena, he disappeared. He stopped coming to me at all, stopped telling me about his day even. The only words that passed between us were the mumbled helloes we exchanged as I walked out the door to work and he came home from his nights spent with her.

A little while after I lost Harry to Ameena, things started to cool between Abdul and me. He had the usual rich guy's attitude toward money: he never had enough of it and he always knew more was coming his way. He borrowed from me. When I was having my own fiscal difficulties, I asked him to pay me back, but he acted like I was joking. When he realized I was serious, he grew colder. He started to refuse to give me shifts at the Kabab Kaiser. When he did give me work, it was the hardest shifts. He promoted another cook, even though I had seniority. Eventually, he stopped taking my calls.

When Abdul and I stopped hanging out, I grew more and more depressed, but I had nobody to talk to. Harry was always with Ameena, and my dad was always working. I started drinking more and using.

Then, Harry came home one evening, crying. He came straight to me. Ameena was talking about going to college in Chicago he told me, sobbing. She thought it was better if they spent less time together after she returned from Guyana.

Harry plopped down on the floor. I pulled out my stash and rolled a joint. We sat together, and I watched as he cried, took a puff, and cried some more. Seeing him curdled all the anger I'd been feeling against Abdul. It wasn't hard to go from loneliness to hate.

Slowly, as we smoked, he stopped crying and together we began to construct the conspiracy. I told Harry about Abdul and how Abdul had screwed me over. Abdul and Ameena were trying to put distance between us. They had always seen us as toys, their version of slumming. Now they were throwing us to the side. As I spoke, Harry deliberated.

"Ameena has a set of keys to the cottage," he said.

"Keys? No way. Abdul wouldn't let anyone else keep those keys."

"He got locked out one time. He gave a spare to Ameena on her life. She's not supposed to carry it with her. She wasn't supposed to show it to anyone. She keeps it under her pillow. We were," he paused, "together." His face grew red and blotchy, and he stammered. "And my hand slipped under her pillow. I felt it."

I sighed. "Well, that's great, thambi. But why tell me this?"

"I'll steal it," he said. "I'll steal it and then we'll be able get in."

"So what? Why would we want to go into that hell hole?"

And that's when it came to me. Our big prank.

I grant I was the one that came up with the plan to leave the turkey bombs in Abdul's cottage, but Harry offered to steal the keys and make a copy. I didn't force him to do a thing. I didn't force him to steal, and I didn't force him to come with me that night. That much I swear, I swear to you.

You got to believe me.

—————

At the hospital the next day, the doctor told us Harry had peptic ulcers. His condition could be controlled with antibiotics. She was going to let Harry go home after a few more tests, but he had to be very careful.

Harry was seated in bed. The color had come back to his face; he even laughed and joked with us. The night before, my father had had me drive the taxi home, grab some clothes for Harry, and take the bus back. I was unpacking the things I'd brought and putting his old clothes away when Ameena called.

When Harry heard her voice, he clutched the cell close to his face and started to coo. I could hear her bawling on the other end. Harry described his ordeal, all the torment he had gone through. He laid it on so thick, even my dad was rolling his eyes. Then all of a sudden, Harry started screaming. *Yes! Yes! Yes!* A nurse came running into the room; my father shooed her away.

When Harry flipped his phone shut, he turned to my dad. "Ameena agreed to marry me."

"Marry!" my father yelped.

Harry talked only to my father; he didn't dare look in my direction. "Before she left for Guyana, I asked her to marry me, but she refused. Now she's changed her mind. She realizes how much she misses and loves me. She's going to marry me!"

My father, I noticed, was turning green, but he didn't say anything. I walked to the window and looked out. A NYPD police van, sirens flashing, scooted down the wrong side of the avenue sending pedestrians and oncoming traffic scattering across the intersection. "Please be happy for me," my brother begged.

The doctor came in and asked to speak to my father in the corridor. When my father was gone, Harry called to me. I pretended not to hear him. "We got to go back," Harry said.

"They won't even know we're involved. You made a copy of the keys and put them back." Harry didn't respond. "You did that. Right? I told you to do that."

"There wasn't time, anna. I wasn't able to see her before she left." He hiccupped and started to sob. "You don't know what it's like to love someone as much as I love Ameena." He wasn't saying this as an accusation but more like a statement of fact. Still, it hurt like all fuck. "There's no one in the world I love more." Even though I wasn't looking in his direction, I could see him, his arms outstretched beseechingly like he used to do when he was little and wanted me to carry him. "Please, let's go back and clean it up."

I put my face against the window. It was surprisingly cool given how warm it was outside. "Sure," I said into the glass, hoping he wouldn't hear me. But from the cheering and clapping, I knew he had.

I remember being with girls Abdul and I picked up. I'd be having sex with them, moving inside them, and suddenly I wouldn't be in my body at all. I'd be floating above them. I'd see their faces twisted in pleasure, and I'd feel gratitude to them, for their bodies, for their per-sonalities, for who they were. But always I'd return, and after it was over, I couldn't imagine how to keep that feeling going. Love is trust, brotherhood, loyalty. Maybe it sounds like one of those stupid bank ads you see on the subway but love is fidelity. But it wasn't my place to tell my little brother that. He had to find out on his own.

For three weeks, my father doted over Harry and, when he was working, he asked my upstairs neighbor to watch over him. Every day, Harry kept bothering me about the turkey bombs. I kept telling him relax. Even in this heat, it would take some time for the jars to explode. After that, Harry started quoting the weather report for that day: nine-ty-eight degrees, one hundred degrees, one hundred and two degrees.

Eventually, I gave in. I was sure my brother's pestering was going to make him even more ill, so late one evening we went back to Abdul's. I offered to go on my own, being that he was sick and all, but for some reason my brother wanted to accompany me. I suspected, though he never said as much, that he didn't trust me.

We were halfway across the yard when a spotlight trained on Harry. I tried to pull him away but he wouldn't move. Then the light swung away, toward the Ukrainians' house. "The Ukrainians have floodlights in their yard," I observed, stupidly.

"There's been a few break-ins in this neighborhood," my brother replied.

"Word." I gave him a look and we both burst out laughing. The first time we'd laughed together in a long time.

When we opened the cottage, the stench hit us immediately. Harry dropped to his knees, gagging.

I pulled my t-shirt over my face and looked around. Four of the jars still stood, glistening and pristine in the light of the Ukrainian's floods. But all that was left of the fifth jar was the bottom, a perfectly round disc of glass, sitting on the floor of the cottage. The force of the explosion had propelled rotten turkey juice onto the bed, on the stereo and television, on the floor. The cheap wood the cottage was made of had absorbed some of the goop. Abdul was never going to get it out. I mean if I'd really wanted this to work, I would have gone to the store and purchased me some Liquid ASS. It was supposed to be a joke: a message, that I could reach Abdul if I wanted. But this was bad. Whatever, Abdul had done, he hadn't deserved this.

My brother let out a long, low whimper. "How are we going to clean it up, anna?"

"Let's get the jars out and tomorrow I'll come back with some—?"

Harry shushed me. "Did you hear that? There's someone at the fence."

As soon as he spoke, we heard loud whispering from next door followed by muffled footsteps.

My brother gawked, terrified; his lower jaw flapped up and down but no sound came. He looked horrible, like one of those laughing skeletons at the haunted house. That image sobered me. I knew what had to happen. I walked over to the window and opened it, in case the Ukrainians were watching the door. I gestured for him to get out. When he crawled through, he offered his hand to me. I shook my head.

"What? Come on, we got to go."

"If I stay, you'll be able to get away easier."

Harry studied the street, then studied my face. He handed me the keys to the cottage. "You won't be able to explain how you got in without them," he said.

I stared at him. Was it that easy to give me up? His only brother. And what was the point any way? No way Ameena wasn't going to figure out that he was the one who stole the keys.

But, as I felt the weight of the keys, the metal against the flesh of my palm, I knew I'd do anything for him, even if that anything didn't make a whole lot of sense. "Gee, thanks," I mumbled. But he didn't stick around long enough to notice the sarcasm—or the sadness—in my voice.

I watched Harry sprint across the yard and vault the fence at the far end of the yard. He didn't look back.

A few minutes later, someone called in heavily accented English for me to come out. I opened the door slowly. Three Ukrainian's stood, shotguns pointed at my head. A girl, she couldn't be more than ten, was pointing a Mag-lite in my direction. I held my hands above my head. "Don't shoot!" I called out, wishing to hell I could speak Ukrainian.

I heard sirens approaching. Over the top of the hedges, I saw a pair of flashing lights turn the corner and approach Abdul's house. The Ukrainians still held their shotguns on me, but they didn't look as tense as before. I guessed they weren't going to shoot me as long as I kept my hands up. As the police cars screeched to a halt in front of Abdul's house, I ran my finger over the sharp edge of Ameena's keys and reviewed my story, so I'd get it right the first time. I gripped those keys tight between my fingers.

I held on as the cops bounded across the yard, guns drawn, and forced me onto my stomach. I held on as one officer shoved my face into the grass and the other handcuffed me. I held on even as I began to gag on the dirt and the grass filling my mouth. I only let go when the cop snatched the keys from my fingers. The only thing I hoped was Ameena wouldn't blame Harry for his fuck-up brother. But I wasn't really worried. If she felt even an iota of the love I felt for Harry that moment the cops yanked me from the ground and pushed me in the direction of the squad car, she would never let him go.

The Demon

Shila's grandson Ganesh curled back his upper lip and exposed two long demon fangs. Within hours, villagers began arriving at the house. They crouched around Ganesh, sarongs and saris pulled up between their thighs, and peered into his face. As Shila watched in disgust, the fools pointed to her grandson's fangs, spoke all sorts of rubbish about raksha and yakka—demons and ghosts—and gave money either from fear or for luck. A reporter from a Colombo newspaper came. He talked briefly to Ganesh and then asked to examine the fangs. Ganesh refused. This confirmed what Shila already suspected. She'd given a pair of costume fangs to Ganesh as a gift five years ago, when she'd returned to Sri Lanka from North Carolina. He must have kept them hidden some place, and Shila's son and his wife had forgotten about them.

Ganesh was too young—he was only sixteen—to be so sick. As a child he had been playful and curious—a normal boy. While she was working in North Carolina, Shila's son, Ranji, had sent her photographs of Ganesh making faces, contorting his features in improbable ways, to elicit a laugh; she kept these photographs—yellowing in the corners, color already fading—in a little album stashed among her few belongings. Over the past year, Ganesh had grown sullen and uncooperative. A few months before donning the fangs, he complained of nightmares, heard voices nobody else could hear, and spoke to people nobody else could see. Even though Shila had attended school for only a few years, she knew this was a sickness because she had heard the North Carolina mahatteya and hami—the couple for whom she had worked thirteen years as an ayah—speaking of such illnesses. They were doctors, and the people they treated saw and spoke of the kind of things Ganesh saw and spoke of now. They also spoke of a medicine that made these people better.

Shila had not mentioned any of this to her son Ranji. Shila had a place to live only because of her son, and she did not want to give him a reason to ask her to leave.

Shila did not know her age because her father had applied for her birth certificate many years after she was born, but she knew she was not old. No more than fifty-two. Still, her hair had gone completely white and her face, once beautiful, now appeared formless, nothing but the intersection of grooves, crevices, and shadows. More and more she had to chew gum made from the milk of an unripe papaw to ease the aching of her gums and teeth. She steeped gotu kola leaves and drank the broth to help the swelling in her ankles and the dark spots appearing on the skin of her hands.

And she was alone. Shila's husband, a Tamil, had been killed twenty years ago during the riots. This was before the war between the army and the Tigers. Her friends claimed a bad horoscope, an evil eye cast on her, or just her bad luck caused her husband's death. She learned the only way to stop these comments was to remain silent. She was a tiny woman, lean and wiry, and she used her size to disappear into her surroundings.

A few days later, early in the morning before Shila had finished combing her hair, she heard a car honking and the rattle of the gate as her daughter-in-law opened it. Shila watched as her daughter-in-law waved the car to the end of the driveway underneath a frangipani tree, golden blossoms quivering like tiny flames. A young couple Shila recognized got out of the car followed by a blond-haired woman she did not know. They spoke briefly to Shila's daughter-in-law, who led them into the house.

The couple came not from the village, but from Colombo. They owned a beach bungalow close by, which they visited a few weekends a year. During that time, the husband had come to Ranji, a mechanic, for help with his car or small repairs around the house. A year ago, Ranji had sent Ganesh to work for the couple, and they'd continued to pay Shila's grandson a small fee to do odd jobs around their compound. Shila hoped the couple had come to help the boy, to give the name perhaps of a Colombo doctor.

Ganesh was already in the sitting room. He was slouched in a chair, head lolling to the side. Tall and lean, Ganesh might have looked like any sixteen-year-old except for the two ivory tips peeking from behind his top lip. Ranji was seated beside him. When Ranji saw the couple and their woman friend, he jumped up and crouched before them touching their feet.

Ranji's greeting surprised Shila. Through his own resources and business acumen, her son had prospered as a car mechanic. He had even gone to Saudi Arabia for two years and had brought back an even larger pot of money than he'd left with. He greeted even the wealthiest clients with a slight, backward tilt of his head; they had come to him, after all, for his expertise. Watching Ranji now led Shila to hope even more strongly that the couple had come to give advice.

Ranji brought chairs for the trio, and they sat in front of her grandson. Ganesh stared past them and did not reply when the young man tried to speak to him. The couple and their friend made a show of being grateful when the daughter-in-law offered them tea. They sat quietly, seeming more interested in their cups than in the boy. The husband finally goaded their friend, an American visiting for a few weeks, to take a photograph of Ganesh.

"Have you called a kattadiya?" the man asked Ranji. "That's an exorcist," he explained softly to the blond-haired woman. He was heavyset with a ruddy, blotched complexion like the skin of a pomegranate. His face seemed to crack when he smiled. "That would be quite a specta-cle. To have an exorcism here."

"Oh yes," cooed his wife. "Emily would come back to see that. Wouldn't you?"

"Sure," replied their friend, trying to juggle the camera and her tea-cup. "But maybe, if you haven't yet, you should consult a doctor too?"

"Sometimes the village doctor accompanies the exorcist," he said. While the friend positioned herself to take a picture of the boy, he pulled out his wallet and handed Ranji a bundle of rupee notes. "Thank you for letting us come. We saw the article and thought this would be an opportunity to show Emily life in a Sri Lankan village." Shila's heart sank when Ranji accepted the money.

Ranji led the couple and their friend out of the sitting room. They stood in the garden talking to each other too far away for Shila to hear. Suddenly the young man and her son looked over at Shila. Frightened, she stepped back into the shadow. Ranji shook his head as if in response to a question that he had asked.

Shila tried to calm her racing heartbeat. Did her son suspect her of being involved in Ganesh's illness? Did he remember, after all, about the vampire fangs? But as Ranji walked up the veranda, he said noth-ing. He did not look angry or suspicious. He simply ignored her as he usually did.

"There is a way we can help the boy," Shila called to Ranji as he passed. "If you will listen to me, I can tell you what we have to do."

Ranji stopped but did not turn toward Shila. "I have been with this boy all his life," he replied. "You have not. I will be the one who finds a way to help him."

Shila walked back into the sitting room and stood to the side watch-ing Ganesh. She wondered if her grandson was trying to fool them in some way. It even occurred to her Ranji was in on the deception somehow. There was no other way to explain her son's willingness to take the money offered by the couple. But, as she watched, her grand-son stared ahead, mumbling to himself, talking the gibberish he had spouted off and on for a year. The boy grew angry and began stabbing the air with his finger. Shila realized Ganesh was talking angrily with someone who did not exist.

⊶ ⊰⊱ ⊷

There were days Shila did not think of how her husband died. Then there were other days—when the reports about the civil war came over the television or her son related a new rumor of more fighting—that her loss crept into her body like a rheumatism and seeped into her joints. Those days her heart would swell into her throat and press so tight against her chest she thought each rib would snap, one by one.

After her husband's death, without anyone to support her, Shila had had to find a job that would provide her with the money she and her husband had once earned together. Shila could earn far more overseas than in Sri Lanka, so when she was offered a post with a Sri Lankan couple in North Carolina, she took it. Ranji was fourteen when she left and had begged her not to go. It was, he had said, like losing two parents at once. And now, even though she had sent Ranji a portion of her income every month, there existed a distance between them. He offered her only what was required of him. He had allowed her to live with him and his family for the past five years, but he made it clear he had never forgiven her for going to the States. If she could do nothing for Ranji now, she could at least help Ganesh.

An opportunity to help her grandson finally presented itself when the cook, afraid of the boy no doubt, called and made an excuse not to come. Now her daughter-in-law would have to make the meals, but there was no food. Shila volunteered to go to the kadé, the roadside shacks that hawked produce and other goods. She found the trishaw driver she preferred sitting at the end of the lane chewing betel. His presence made Shila believe even more strongly in the rightness of what she was doing.

She asked the driver to take her to the kadé run by the ja-miniha. The produce there was not cheap, but the quality was good. More

130

importantly, the ja-miniha who owned the place knew people in the village and outside as well. He might be able to give the name of a doctor who could help Ganesh.

She was lucky for the second time that morning because the ja-miniha—not his wife—was sitting in the store. He held out a newspaper as Shila approached. "Your grandson is on page three." He folded the paper to highlight a small article and a photograph of Ganesh—white fangs thrust out from behind his upper lip. Shila barely glanced at it.

"This is why I've come," she said. "Ganesh is ill. You must know of a doctor who can help him."

"What doctor? The boy needs a dentist, no?" The ja-miniha slapped his thighs and grinned. His wide, fleshy lips stretched like a rubber band to the edges of his high, slanting cheekbones.

"The boy has an illness in his head. He needs a doctor."

"Oh, you mean a headshrinker, someone who will talk to him for hours and say how bad his life is."

"There's a medicine. I want a doctor who will give my grandson that medicine."

"Take the boy to the ayurvedics," suggested the ja-miniha. When Shila remained resolute, the ja-miniha leaned forward over the counter. "Listen, madam, do not go to the headshrinkers, to *those* doctors. They will not give your grandson medicine. Medicine is expensive. They will put the boy into a hospital instead." The ja-miniha beckoned Shila closer. "Arumugasamy sent his daughter to one of the government doctors, and they put her in the asylum," he whispered. "Do you know, madam, they sent the daughter home pregnant. The girl told Arumugasamy she was raped by the inmates." He shuddered as he repeated this.

Shila felt a crescent of pain, sharp and urgent, tug at her belly, but before she could reply the ja-miniha shook his head. "There is nothing to be done for your grandson," he said as he stood up. "Ganesh is not hurting anyone. He is not hurting himself. He even makes a little money for your family. Just let him go on like this until he gets tired of it." The ja-miniha returned to his newspaper. "My recommendation, madam," he said as she walked out the door, "Let him be."

On the ride back to her house, the trishaw driver jabbered away, asking questions about Ganesh. Shila tried politely to ignore him, to stare at the immutable stretch of white sky. She was relieved when they were forced to stop for a small perahera welcoming a new Buddhist monk to the local temple. The driver quieted, and she was able to watch the parade. Children dressed in white and carrying sticks topped with colored streamers headed the procession. Two drummers marched behind keeping a slow, steady beat meant to ward off the raksha. Townspeople and monks followed.

The monks dressed in saffron, gold, or burgundy robes, weaving silently back and forth, reminded Shila of autumn leaves caught in the wind. She felt a sudden longing for fall—the seasons would be turning soon in North Carolina—for cold, dry air and the smell of cured tobacco, pine needles, the feel of sandy earth instead of recalcitrant clay.

She thought of the little boy and girl she had looked after in North Carolina. One October, a few weeks before Shila returned to Sri Lanka, the children had wanted to dress up as vampires for Halloween. They looked very silly and adorable in their costumes, and they very much liked their vampire fangs. Shila had meant only to buy a frivolous, meaningless gift for Ganesh. She had been sure the costume fangs were something any child, especially a mischievous boy who liked to make faces, would enjoy.

After the perahera passed, while the trishaw driver waited for the line of cars ahead to begin moving, a young beggar, wild-eyed and stinking of alcohol, thrust his hand into the trishaw. The driver tried to beat him away as Shila pressed against the leather seat to avoid his probing hands. She recognized the beggar. He was an ex-soldier who'd fought in Jaffna and had gone mad after his return. His family, unable to control him, had banished him from the house. The driver finally pushed the beggar away, and the beggar loped toward the other cars. As Shila stared after him through the rear window of the trishaw, she thought of Ganesh.

When Shila returned, Ranji was waiting for her in the kitchen. "I have called the kattadiya," he said. "He will come at the end of the week. We will have to do a lot of preparation. People from the village will come to watch, and they will expect food. You will help cook, no?" Shila nodded her head, but when she tried to speak, to tell her son the truth about the costume fangs, her throat felt coated with straw. Her voice was nothing more than a thick, dry rasp. When she didn't respond, her son continued, "There is something else I want to talk to you about."

Shila tried again to respond but again all that came was a tired croak.

"What is wrong with you?" her son demanded. "You are acting strange lately. You are ill?" Ranji peered at Shila suspiciously. "What I have to say can wait. Till you feel better."

Shila did not believe in demons. When she was born the astrologers had declared her a rakshasa gana, a select person able to see and ward off the spirits, demons, and ghosts who haunted people's lives, wreaking havoc. But Shila's experience only confirmed such things did not really exist. People claimed to see the demons only when it was convenient, and the kattadiya seemed useful only as a way to scare people into behaving.

Shila had witnessed only one exorcism in her life, many years before when she was still young and newly married. The family of a young girl caught with a village boy held an exorcism at their house to cure the girl. Shila had seen her and her friends, lithe and pretty in their white school uniforms, marching arm in arm every morning down the lane on which Shila lived. Shila went to the exorcism because she was curious about the girl and because, back then, she had still wanted to believe.

The kattadiya had arrived with cohorts dressed in their scarlet and white dancing costumes, sporting intricately carved demon masks. The masks depicted demons, half animal, half bird, with huge protuberant eyes. Cobras curved around feral beaks. The kattadiya started by chanting. As the day progressed and the crowd grew more frenzied, the kattadiya struck the girl in the face hard enough to knock her down. The blow propelled Shila back into the crowd as if she were the one struck, and she ran home, afraid to stay and see what else happened. After the exorcism, Shila no longer saw the girl walking along the street and when Shila inquired later about her, she was told the girl had only lost a tooth. Little matter about the tooth, the father explained. The girl was much quieter and ready to listen.

This village's kattadiya was a fool, in Shila's estimation. But he was a fool capable of striking Ganesh. Ganesh was not a teenage girl caught kissing a boy, but a strong, young man. And Shila knew, if someone tried to hurt him, he would fight back.

Shila spent the day finishing household chores. Every time she tried to bring herself to tell Ranji about the costume fangs she remembered the way he had looked at her when speaking to the young man from Colombo. Finally, in the evening, when everyone else had gone to sleep, she steeled herself and went to him.

Ranji was at his desk in the sitting room, hunched over a ledger reconciling some figures. When he saw her approach, he smiled faintly but kindly. Her son's smile heartened Shila, made her sure about what she wanted to say.

"I have something to ask you," said Shila's son. "The man from Colombo, the one who came today wanted to know if you—"

"No," said Shila quietly. "Let me explain first."

"What?" Ranji asked with a sigh. "Explain what?"

Shila took a deep breath. "I'm responsible for Ganesh. I am the reason he is the way he is." Shila paused. "I gave him the fangs."

The muscle along Ranji's neck and jaw tighten. "I don't understand," he said.

"They are costume fangs. I gave them to Ganesh a long time ago. As a present."

Ranji looked down at his ledger as if he expected to find a response among the columns of numbers. Finally he asked, "Have you told anyone about the costume fangs? You have not mentioned this to anyone?"

"He is sick. You can see this, no?"

"You went to the kadé today." Ranji's voice was urgent and demanding. "Did you tell anyone there?"

"No, I only went to find a name of a doctor, but I did not speak of anything else." Ranji appeared to relax a little. "You will take Ganesh to a doctor now?" Shila asked. "Now that you know he is ill."

"Ill? How is he ill?" Ranji cried. "Tell me what the name of this illness is?" When Shila couldn't answer, he continued. "You want me to take him to the doctor and say the boy has an illness you or I cannot name. People will laugh at me. They will say, 'If he cannot know what costume fangs look like, how can he know the inside of a car engine?' Or worse they will say I tried to trick them." Ranji slammed the table. "If I lose business, who will give you money to live."

"They will not have to know. You can take him to a doctor in Colombo—"

"There are many people coming to see the kattadiya, to see an exorcism. What will they think if I take him to a doctor a few days later? They will say I don't believe, that I'm turning my back on the village." Ranji sat down, his chest and back heaving. "The kattadiya has helped people before. He will be enough to help Ganesh." He did not look at Shila but pretended to study the ledger instead. Shila backed slowly from the room.

It did not surprise Shila that Ranji was angry. She had expected that. But she had also believed that when she told her son about the fangs he would agree to take Ganesh to the doctor. She went to her room, undressed, and lay in her bed. She listened as Ranji paced well into the night.

The next morning, as Shila helped her daughter-in-law cook the meals, Ranji came up to Shila and asked quietly, "You are sure you have told no one?" Shila nodded. The daughter-in-law did not look up from her cooking or act as if she thought the question unusual. Shila wondered if Ranji had already spoken to her.

Ranji announced he was going into the village; he would be back later that afternoon. He grabbed Shila's arm and demanded she not leave the house. When Ranji returned a few hours later, Shila was sitting in the living room next to Ganesh. Ranji pulled up a seat.

"I have good news for you," he began. Shila's heart skipped. Was it possible Ranji had gone to the village and spoken with a doctor? "The man, Fonseka, from Colombo, the one who came yesterday, he wants you to come live with his family and help take care of their child."

For a minute Shila could not breathe; the pain tugged again at her stomach. "I am too old for that," she replied.

"Of course not. In fact, I'm sure living here must be hard on you. Now you'll have your own income. The couple will give you a small room. And you will be in Colombo."

Shila looked down, so that she would not have to look into Ranji's face, and pulled distractedly at her blouse. She noticed that the cuticles of her fingers were raw and bleeding. She tried to remember when she had done something like that to herself. "I do not want to leave you or Ganesh," she said softly.

"This is a good opportunity for you, and, truly, what has happened to Ganesh" Ranji searched for words, "has caused you too much distress. You obviously cannot think straight. You should leave these decisions to me."

Shila looked over at Ganesh and wondered if he understood anything that was happening. She stroked his forearm, but he did not seem to know she was there.

"Here's a bus ticket," Ranji offered. "I will help you pack your things. There is a bus leaving tonight and the Fonsekas will be expecting you." She could not bring herself to look at Ranji as he spoke. Shila did not feel angry or sorry but ashamed. She had tried to ensure another end, but things had still happened as she had expected. "You will be able to come back," Ranji continued. "When they come to stay at the bungalow. And they will, of course, give you vacations." Shila took the bus ticket.

When Ranji left the room, Shila leaned her head against Ganesh's shoulder. She felt the warmth of the blood pumping through his body and the gentle expansion of his chest as he took each breath. But the boy did not respond to her touch in any way.

As a little child, her father told Shila the folk tales about the demons. When he did, he always told her she, more than anyone else, had nothing to fear. She was a rakshasa gana. But even then, Shila thought this some sort of bad joke. If she could see demons and ghosts, this would provide some sort of relief. But there existed nothing around her. Her surroundings were as insubstantial and transient as the tattered prayer flag hung from the Bo tree at the Buddhist temple or the pirith noola tied around the supplicant's wrist. It was not the demons Shila feared but the feeling she was something thatched together, desiccated and flimsy. It took all her effort, all her concentration, to stay on the ground, to keep from being wafted away by the hot, dry wind.

Shila closed her eyes and pressed the side of her face against Ganesh's body searching for the dull thump of the boy's heart. If Shila could only find this, then she would know they were, both of them, still alive.

Treble Seven, Double Naught

C hamika checked her iPhone and discovered several messages from her aunt in Sri Lanka. "We need your help," Chamika's aunt rasped in the last one. Chamika was close to her uncle, her father's youngest brother, but, since leaving Sri Lanka, she had spoken to her uncle a few times a year. She rarely—she could think of only two times in the past decade—spoke to the aunt.

Chamika canceled her plans for the evening so that she could return her aunt's phone call. She ordered takeout because she felt too anxious to cook and watched three hours of television shows, none of which she had watched before or enjoyed now. After the local newscast had finished, Chamika placed the call to Colombo. When her aunt picked up, Chamika started to promise as she always did to transfer money to her uncle's bank account in Sri Lanka. Her uncle had been sick over the past year, and she assumed that her uncle and aunt needed help with his medical bills. But her aunt stopped her. "It is not for us. My brother has asked that I call you. He needs money for his daughter."

"For Amanthi, nenda?" Chamika asked. "Is that who you mean? Amanthi needs money?"

"Yes, Amanthi." Chamika had no blood ties to her aunt's family but had befriended her aunt's niece, Amanthi, in school. The last time Chamika had seen Amanthi was nearly fifteen years before when Amanthi and her husband had first arrived in the States. They had not spoken over the phone for twelve years. What made Chamika even more curious was that her aunt had not used Amanthi's name, had spoken as if she Chamika didn't know her.

"I can give her any money she wants," Chamika offered. "Ask her to call me."

"You are not understanding," the aunt protested. "Amanthi is having some sort of difficulty. My brother would like you to transfer money into her account." Chamika didn't respond. "One thousand dollars," the aunt added. Chamika was used to the family asking for money. She lived in the States. She was single. She did a good job, made a salary in the low six figures. Because she didn't need much herself, because the act was a simple gesture that had an impact, she didn't mind giving the money. The year before she had given nearly three thousand dollars to her uncle, a retired teacher, for his surgery. But Amanthi lived in the States, and she had a husband. Why would Amanthi have need for such a lot of money? And why would she call Sri Lanka asking for such a large amount, nearly one lakh? There seemed something irresponsible, very unlike the Amanthi Chamika had known.

"I will give you the information you need," her aunt informed Chamika in a crisp, businesslike tone. Chamika heard a brief commotion on the other end and then her aunt returned. "The bank is Northern Bank. The daughter's name is Amanthi Gianopoulos. The account number is five, two, four, treble seven, five, double naught, three." It took Chamika a moment—she had been in American that long—to retranslate the treble seven to three sevens and the naughts to zeros. She asked her aunt to repeat the numbers just to be sure she had not misunderstood and wrote it down onto the first piece of paper she could reach: a pink Post-it with a cartoon heart in one corner, a bumble bee, its flight path marked by a trail of dashes, in the other, and the heading "Don't forget to—"

"What has happened to Amanthi?" Chamika's aunt explained that Amanthi's husband had lost a lot of money recently, and Amanthi needed help. As Chamika stared at the account number she felt an instinctual suspicion. She had never liked her aunt or her aunt's siblings. Chamika's family belonged to the Govigama caste and the aunt's family belonged to another. Chamika's paternal uncle was a sweet man but easily taken in. The feeling in the family was the he'd married beneath him. "This doesn't look like a bank account number, nenda?"

"This is what was given," her aunt replied.

"Nenda, I will send the money," she insisted. "Have Amanthi call me."

"If you cannot," the aunt replied tightly, "I will find some other way."

"I'm not worried about the money, or about being paid back." Her aunt already knew as much. "But there are laws in this country, nenda. I cannot transfer money into unknown accounts." She imagined what would happen right after she did that, a call from the FBI, or Immigration, or Homeland Security. She heard stories of deportations for minor infractions. Transferring money into strange accounts must list among them. "I need other information, the routing number for example," Chamika insisted. There was more silence on the other end. "I don't even know where she lives now."

"They are in some city there," her aunt replied. "Vermont. That is the name."

Chamika sighed. "Get Gamini-aiya to call me with the information tomorrow," she said. Gamini was her aunt and uncle's eldest son. He worked for a bank in Colombo. He was the one who had helped Chamika remit money to her uncle's account and if there was anyone who could help, he would. Her aunt agreed reluctantly. "You will be helping her, no?" her aunt demanded.

The reception on Chamika's cell phone faded and her aunt's voice became muffled. Chamika used the moment to apologize and ring off. She stared at the number her aunt had given her. She fished out a checkbook from her purse and compared the numbers. Something was off.

The next day, as Chamika was browsing online, a text box appeared. Gamini was trying to reach her through Skype. Chamika's cousin apologized profusely. "But I want to help," Chamika interrupted.

Her cousin's image popped up in a window in the corner. Chamika could see that he was seated in the bedroom of his apartment in Colombo. Behind him was a set of sliding doors, and behind those Chamika could make out the clay-tiled rooftops of the bungalows next door, of coconut palms, and of a crescent of shoreline. Chamika experienced a swift pang of nostalgia; her voice caught in her throat.

"Amma should have not have involved you in this," Gamini said.

"But what is wrong, aiya?"

"Nothing is wrong," her cousin said too quickly and with a forced breeziness.

"Amanthi and her husband are having financial problems?"

Gamini lowered his voice. "She is not having problems. She is just trying to worry her father. She knows that none of us here have that kind of money."

"Have you spoken with her?"

"I don't need to. She has always been this way. A very cruel girl." This struck Chamika as wrong. She remembered Amanthi as a timid girl who had done whatever she was told. She had decorated her room with posters of angels and kittens and unicorns and had copied in her notebooks aphorisms that exhorted her to love herself and others. It was Chamika that the family described as cruel. "Amma over-reacted when she heard about the call," the cousin continued. "I have reminded her of what that girl is capable of, and amma agrees. There is no need for any of us to be sending money."

"You can't be serious, aiya? You're not even going to try and help Amanthi?"

"She is playing pucks with us," Gamini insisted. "Two years we hear nothing. She never calls. Only sends a Christmas card. Then after such a silence, she phones out of nowhere."

"Maybe there's something wrong, aiya."

Her cousin pursed his lips. "It surprises me you care so much."

When she asked why, he replied, "You, Chamika-nangi, are not exactly overflowing with the milk of human kindness." He punctuated this with a tight laugh meant she knew to make it seem as if he had just made a joke. She was used to this kind of petty nastiness from certain family members. Her cousin believed his mother's version of Chamika.

"I give money," she pointed out. "I have given every time anyone there has asked."

Gamini shrugged. "It is just that. Money."

"It is not just money when you need it," she replied.

The subject of Amanthi clearly no longer interested her cousin. Gamini ended the video feed. "Unless she calls to explain herself, we are not going to help her. You are not to help her either"

Chamika sat back in her chair. "Is that a command, aiya?"

"I am asking you, nangi, to stay out of something that isn't your business," offered the disembodied voice. "But you have always done what you wanted," He wished Chamika well and ended the call.

· ·—·≈·≈·—· ·

Chamika had arrived in the States in the early Nineties. When the government closed the universities in Sri Lanka, she applied to Mount Holyoke in Massachusetts and was accepted. She worked now as a physician's assistant at a wealthy plastic surgery practice in Westchester. In her mid-twenties, after a string of relationships with men and women, she had recognized that she was a lesbian. She was open about her sexuality with Americans. She thought of herself as focused but fun loving, free-spirited and independent. She was convinced her friends saw her the same way. She didn't allow herself to think deeper than that. There was a sinkhole you fell into if you thought too long and too hard about yourself.

Amanthi had been a cautious, quiet girl. She and Chamika had attended the same school and belonged to the same circle of friends. Still, despite the family connection, Chamika and Amanthi's

142

relationship had never been a true friendship. Instead, Chamika and Amanthi were more like sisters: one, older and more self-assured, tolerating the younger, more enthusiastically adoring sibling. They were very different. Chamika was spirited and brave; Amanthi placid and reliable. Chamika had been far too concerned with her own life, going with boys, defying her parents, to form a strong bond with a girl like Amanthi.

The day after her conversation with Gamini, Chamika went to the bank. She was friends with one of the accounts managers—the manager often helped Chamika file her overseas remittances. Chamika stopped by the manager's cubicle and showed her the number. The manager studied it. She began typing on her computer. She informed Chamika that there was no Northern Bank in Vermont but there was a TD Banknorth. When Chamika pressed her about the number, the manager demurred. "I can't," she replied. "There are privacy laws. I can't give out that kind of information without a very good reason."

When Amanthi had become engaged to a foreign engineer working in Sri Lanka, the aunt had lorded the impending marriage over Chamika and her family. Amanthi was marrying a well-educated and successful white man. Chamika was twenty-five and lived in the States and was not yet married. Worse, it was rumored she was a lesbian. She had never denied the rumors—it was true after all—but she had never outed herself to her family. That was an American cultural ritual, and they would hear what they needed to know from Sri Lankans living in the States. She had nothing to prove to them. Chamika had made some excuse that she was sitting for exams and had skipped the wedding. Amanthi called when she and her husband arrived in the States, and they'd met for dinner at a hotel in Manhattan. The husband had not impressed Chamika. This was not the person Chamika had imagined when her aunt had told her Amanthi was marrying a handsome Greek man. He wasn't young and strapping—in other words an Adonis. Instead he was unnaturally pale, at least a stone overweight, and nearly two decades older than Amanthi. Chamika might have forgiven these deficiencies if he had proven to be charming or kind. But

Amanthi's husband had acted tetchy the entire dinner. Chamika had detected little love between the couple and it had occurred to Chamika that Amanthi had married solely to escape her family and Sri Lanka.

Chamika went home and looked for her cousin on Facebook but couldn't find a profile under her cousin's name. She twittered— PRT@Chamisaok any1 hear from cozin Amanthi? LMK ASAP. A few friends retweeted her post but Chamika heard nothing else. She typed Amanthi's full name into Google. She came up with one listing under Amanthi Gianopoulos. The listing gave Amanthi's age, described her as married, no children. She discovered that her cousin worked as a secretary at a law firm in a town in Vermont. She took down the firm's number. She typed in the husband's last name. There was only one man living in the town with that last name. A Christos Gianopoulos. The link led her to the web page of the local university where he was faculty, a professor of engineering. She found another link to an article he'd co-authored a few years ago. Another link took her to an article in a newspaper. There was no mention anywhere of Amanthi. Finally, she used the reverse lookup. She was able to find the address easily but the phone number was blocked. She printed the information and tacked it to the board underneath the unidentified bank account number.

* * *

Chamika was surprised when her acquaintances, her patients, her lovers referred to her as American. She once had caught the pastor of her church off guard by reminding him that she was a Sri Lankan. He had looked confused and then had started to explain, "But you're so . . ." He thought better of whatever it was he was going to say and changed the subject. He never finished his thought. There was no question for Chamika. She had never stopped being a Sri Lankan. She never would.

She went to the Sri Lanka Society's gatherings. Despite the fact that she was Christian, she traveled to the Buddhist vihara in Hollis to meditate every Wednesday. It was far easier to be Sri Lankan in America than it had ever been in Sri Lanka. All she had dreamed of as a child was fleeing her parents, the nosy, bossy aunties and uncles, the constant meddling in her life, the pressure to be married and to have children. There you were bound by far too many social obligations; you were always doing things for people. Here, she maintained her freedom while also praising the culture and tradition and telling stories about how wonderful her childhood was. She could rave about home, the cooking, the parties, the people, and nobody knew enough about Sri Lanka to contradict her or cared enough to grill her.

After a few hours of searching, Chamika finally found stashed in her attic in a plastic storage bin an old address book with a cell phone number for Amanthi. When Chamika dialed, the call went straight to voicemail. Chamika left a message that she was sorry to bother Amanthi after such a long time but she had heard Amanthi was having some trouble and wanted to help if possible. When she didn't hear again, she called a third time and left another message. She received a call a few days later. It was a man—someone young, Chamika guessed from the high-pitched quaver in his voice. "Look, I'm calling you because I can tell you're worried about your friend. But you got the wrong number."

"Can you tell me how long you've had this number?" Chamika asked.

The boy hesitated. Chamika knew that he was wondering if Chamika might be conning him. That was one thing Sri Lankans and Americans shared: a deep suspicion of strangers in need. "Two years at least," he finally admitted.

She looked at the number her aunt had given her. The only Northern Bank was in Ireland. Chamika tried looking up phone scams based in Ireland but found nothing that matched. It might not have been an account. Maybe it was a telephone number. But 524 didn't match any known area code, though 52 was the international country code for Mexico. This last fact seemed significant, at first, to Chamika. Later, she dismissed it as coincidence. That evening, Chamika wrote her cousin Gamini to let him know he had the wrong phone number for Amanthi. Did he have another one? The next morning she hadn't heard from

Gamini. She called the law firm that listed Amanthi as an employee. The woman who answered the phone informed her that no person by that name currently worked for them. Chamika asked for the manager. The manager politely informed her that for legal reasons she could only say that Amanthi no longer worked at the firm. "Please, can you tell me? Did she leave two years ago? I am family."

The manager hesitated. "As I said, for legal reasons we don't give out information about present or former employees."

Chamika never heard from her cousin Gamini. She finally broke down and charged the fee for reverse look up and found a phone number for Christos Gianopoulos. She called that weekend. When Chamika asked for Amanthi, the man on the other end informed her immediately that she had the wrong number.

"Christos?" Chamika asked. She gave Christos her name. "I met you a few years ago."

There was a long pause on the other end. "Of course, of course, I'm so sorry. You know these connections. It's sometimes hard to hear." This man had a light twang, the remnant of a Brooklyn or Queens accent. She had always thought Amanthi's husband was Greek—that was what Amanthi's aunt had claimed—but Chamika realized now he had probably grown up in New York City. Had she really not noticed that before about him?

"Can I speak with Amanthi?"

"She's not here." He answered too quickly and there was an edge to his voice.

"When will she be back? I'll call back."

"You know she's in and out." He hesitated. "Can I ask why you're calling?"

"I haven't talked to her in years, and I just wanted to know how she is." There was a long silence on the other end.

"She keeps her own schedule," he replied "How about you leave her your number, and I'll have her call you back?" Chamika gave Christos her information but had a feeling she wouldn't hear anything. When she tried the number again a week later, a message informed her the line had been disconnected.

A month passed. It was mid-October. Chamika was busy at work, and she might have forgotten all about Amanthi if she hadn't one day been looking for a phone number and found still tacked to her board, under a pair of receipts, the mystery code. 5247775003. Gamini had never emailed her back. Chamika guessed Amanthi had not called again demanding the money so they were all of them proven in what they had believed. They were content to wait for the Christmas card. She mentioned the mystery to her girlfriend—a woman she had met in a bar in Jersey City and had started dating recently. She showed her the number. Chamika's girlfriend listened attentively and politely and then joked she should ask that famous television show—the one with all the murders—to investigate. No one has been murdered, Chamika had replied, trying to keep her voice even.

"But something has got to be wrong," the girlfriend had replied after some thought. "You said she's not the kind of person who asks for things. And a thousand dollars? That's a chunk of money. That's an I'm-in-a-lot-of-trouble amount of money. If it were you, wouldn't you want to know someone cared you had disappeared? Especially as a woman."

"Because she's a woman she should know how to take care of herself," Chamika replied. Her girlfriend had peered at her through slitted eyes, her expression stony.

But Chamika did not believe she was wrong. She had come from a much harder culture than any of her American girlfriends, and all there had ever been for Chamika was to be strong. After all Amanthi had lived through—a civil war that had lasted most of her childhood and her adulthood—how was it possible that she could come all this way to America and be in such trouble?

The next day Chamika took out a map and judged the distance between her home and the town in Vermont where Amanthi lived. She had never been to Vermont, but she heard it was lovely in the fall. Chamika did some research and picked the date of a local fall festival. She made plans for a weekend stay in the town where Amanthi lived. She would take a chance. She would drop by Amanthi's house briefly, just to say hello.

The address she had led her to a gray sidesplit on a neatly kept but cramped suburban street not far from the university. The garden was elaborately landscaped with a cobblestone walkway and flowerbeds now winter-barren and adorned with an abundance of lawn ornaments—frolicking wood nymphs, angels, and stone frogs of varying sizes. An American flag hung above the doorway. Chamika stared at the garden surprised by the overabundance of kitsch, out of place in this otherwise tastefully decorated upper middle-class neighborhood. She recognized Amanthi was responsible and the idea that her cousin would still, at this point in their lives, indulge a childhood aesthetic moved Chamika a little. It also reassured her. She could rule out one possibility because surely, if Christos had murdered Amanthi two years ago, he'd have cleaned up this front lawn by now.

Chamika rang the doorbell. The man who opened the door was at least an inch taller than the Christos of Chamika's memory and, though late middle-aged, more muscular and trim. This man could, in fact, be described as handsome.

"Chamika?" Christos's eyes opened wide. "What's happened?" he whispered and she thought, though it made little sense, that he looked terrified. "Why are you here?"

"I'm here to see Amanthi." She tried to sound nonchalant. "I called a while back but no one returned my call so I thought I'd put a visit." She tried to grin.

He shook himself and looked past her as if expecting someone else to be standing behind her. He looked back at her. "It's a surprise." He paused a beat. "A pleasant one of course."

He stepped to the side so that she could enter the house. He led her through a short hallway into the kitchen. "You know Chamika," Christos pronounced her name without hesitation, the way a Sri Lankan would, putting the stress on the first syllable. "Amanthi is out of town. Visiting friends in California."

Christos led Chamika to a long counter and pulled out a stool for her. He offered her a cup of coffee. "I wish you'd called," he said as he poured the remains of a large, glass coffeepot into two mugs. "I could have told you this and saved you the trouble."

Chamika took the mug from Christos. "You have disconnected the number."

Christos cursed to himself. "Of course. I'm sorry about that." Christos exhibited the puffiness around the eyes and the slackness at the jaw line that came with age but his Bob Marley t-shirt was tight enough to reveal a broad muscular chest and a tapering waist. His hair was streaked with gray. The color of his eyes surprised Chamika most. They were blue. She would have sworn the Christos she met had brown eyes. "And she was supposed to call you back I know but things got crazy with her going to California and all." He took a sip of his coffee. "Still, this is a long way to come. I'm surprised."

"We are really worried. Especially after her phone call." He appeared not to understand. "Her phone call to her father. You knew she called, no? A few weeks ago."

"How many weeks ago?"

"Six, I think."

Christos appeared puzzled. "No, I didn't know." He breathed deep. "What did she say?"

"She called her father and said you are having financial trouble. You need money."

Christos snorted. "Yeah, I'm sure *that* worried her father. He's usually the one asking for money." Christos looked around the kitchen. "I don't know why she called. We don't need money. We have plenty . . . or enough." He leaned forward and propped both elbows on the counter so that his head was level with Chamika's. Christos exhaled slowly. "You sure her dad isn't trying to scam you guys?"

Chamika had wondered that herself when her aunt had first called. "The thing is we're worried," she replied.

"We? Who's we?" His tone was slightly annoyed but the truth was Chamika was surprised by how affable Christos was acting. She was an intruder, after all.

"Her family."

Christos smiled slightly and Chamika was struck again that he must have been beautiful when he was young. He still exuded an easy-going sexuality. The kind of man who was aware he was attractive but ambivalent about it. "Her *family* is worried?"

"That's surprising," Christos observed, "because her family hasn't cared enough to call for a long time now." He snorted. "When was the last time we saw you?"

"I'm sorry that I lost contact. And I would like to see Amanthi-nangi again."

Chamika fished through her purse and pulled out the slip of paper with the number on it. She handed it to Christos. "She gave her father this number. I think it's a bank account? But it doesn't match a known bank."

He looked at it. "This isn't our account," he finally replied. He stared at the paper a little longer before handing it back to her.

He straightened and took the mug from Chamika but when he saw it was still half-full slid it back toward her. "Like I said. She's in California visiting friends. Some Sri Lankans. Maybe you know them? She calls them . . ." Christos jabbed a finger in her direction, "you know."

"Batchmates."

He walked over to the sink and placed both mugs in it. "She's visiting batchmates. I can have her call you."

"You could give me her number."

He shook his head. "No, I can't," he said. He stared out the window when he spoke. "She tried for a long time to reach out to you, and she was really hurt when you didn't call her back." He paused. "You know, she was the one that cared about you. When she heard that you were

150

dating women, she tried to call. To let you know it didn't matter to her. Then, she figured you had just cut off all ties." The words themselves were harsh, but his tone was remarkably gentle. "So I think that what I'll do now is this. I'm going to give Amanthi your number and have her call you when she's ready."

Christos suddenly stared into the sink, his expression one of sheer, pathetic devastation. The slip was momentary but pronounced. A man barely holding a deep anguish at bay. There was a story here deeper than a family insult. It was personal and most likely none of Chamika's business. But she wanted to hear that from Amanthi.

By the time Christos looked in Chamika's direction again, he had managed to re-invoke his former affability. He chatted with her about where she was staying. He told her what restaurants to go to in town. The best Thai. The best Indian. He explained that if he'd known she was in town that he would have taken her to dinner, but he had already made plans. He gave her his cell number if she needed anything.

Christos led her to the doorway. When he shook her hand, she was struck again by the thought that Christos was someone easy to like. As she walked toward her car, Chamika wondered how she had possibly gotten Amanthi's husband so wrong.

⋯⋯

As she replayed their conversation, Chamika decided that Christos's demeanor must have been a charade to throw her off. He had been too kind. She had shown up out of nowhere, and he had let her into his house. She had questioned him as if he might be guilty of something. Any normal man would have been, should have been, angry. But throw her off of what?

She decided to eat an early dinner at the Indian restaurant. When she left the restaurant, she noticed the mannequin in the window of the thrift store next door. It was wearing a sari. The sari had been inexpertly wrapped by someone who had seen a sari worn before but had had not known how to drape one.

She entered the store. A young woman standing at the front desk greeted her with a smile and a wave. Chamika browsed through the racks of worn, discarded clothing. The clothes were neatly folded, hung and classified only by size. She had made her way through two racks of jeans and slacks when she found what she had come into the store looking for: three blouses batiked and hand embroidered in a style common to Sri Lanka and a row of saris. She was fingering one of the saris when the shop clerk appeared next to her asking if she could help. "Do you know who left these?" Chamika asked. The clerk shrugged. "You must not get saris often?"

"There's a bunch of Indians who work for the university," the clerk replied. "And people in the community like to buy them. The fabric is good for decorating." Chamika found a label still attached to one sari. The label was for a sari shop in Colombo.

"Do you have a lot of Sri Lankans in the community?" The clerk stared at her blankly. She probably hadn't heard of Sri Lanka before. Chamika turned her attention back to the sari. Most likely, it had never been worn or the owner would have cut the label away. Amanthi took the sari from the rack. "I'd like to buy this."

The clerk pointed to a vitrine at the front of the store. "We have some cool Indian jewelry up front," the clerk added. "There's some really great stuff."

Chamika recognized the jewelry immediately: a silver crochet necklace tipped with beads of amethysts, a matching pair of earrings, and a ring. Amanthi's grandmother had identical jewelry handmade for all of her grandchildren. The jewelry was elaborate but inexpensive, costume jewelry mostly, but they had meant something to the grandmother. Amanthi couldn't have made much money from the set at a place like this thrift shop. The jewelry had been dumped by someone who had wanted to get rid of the items quickly; someone who didn't even care enough to try and profit. Chamika circled the glass case. The last piece was a pendant, a silver cursive 'A' with a garnet set in the right stem. Chamika owned a matching 'C,' a gift from their uncle and aunt on their eighteenth birthdays. Chamika bought the sari and the pendant.

When they had both been teenagers, Chamika and Amanthi and their boyfriends had skipped school and gone to Majestic Cinema instead. This was during the height of the civil war when it seemed as if a bombing occurred nearly every week. Midway through the film, a group of muscular, tattooed men, heads shaved, wearing camouflage pants, entered the theater. They looked like JVPers. The men found seats in the front and watched the movie quietly but Chamika had wondered what might happen if some violence took place. Her body would be found there with her friends, and her parents would know then that she had spent the afternoons with boys. They would not only be sad at her death; they would be ashamed. The image of her parents' humiliation had amused her a little. Better to be the one committing the hurt then the one being hurt. She looked over at Amanthi and recognized that Amanthi was experiencing the entirely opposite reaction. She was sitting arms wrapped around her torso, shivering, leaning away from the boy next to her. Amanthi had noticed the camouflage men as well. And now her defiance was making Amanthi miserable; she had, after all, most likely only come to please Chamika.

The next morning Chamika called in sick to work. She drove to the town's police station. When she told the secretary seated at the front desk that she wanted to report a relative missing he took her contact information and asked her to wait. Ten minutes later a man in a suit walked up to her and introduced himself as a detective. She followed him through the station to his desk.

The detective explained the procedure for filing a missing persons report. As he spoke to her, Chamika became increasingly aware of how silly she was being. She didn't even know what Amanthi looked like now. She couldn't tell the detective if Amanthi had long hair or short, if she had put on or pulled down. She couldn't offer a photograph. She told the detective about the phone call and about her conversation with Christos. She told him about the jewelry. She even showed him the now heavily creased sticky note with the number. The bumblebee had been ripped away and the top of the words 'Don't' and 'Forget' looked like they'd been chewed on. As they spoke, the detective's demeanor shifted from professional concern to amateur psychother-apist—a role, Chamika realized, that was by now well-rehearsed. He explained patiently that he understood Chamika's concern. The department took seriously any report of a missing person, but an adult had the legal right to cut herself off from her family. It was horrible and cruel—he himself didn't understand the motivation—but it hap-pened. After she left the station, Chamika went straight to her motel.

The call from Christos came late morning as Chamika checked out of her bed and breakfast. She had picked up because she thought it might be Amanthi or the detective. "What the fuck, Chamika?" Christos demanded. "You called the police. The police? What the hell did I do to deserve that?" But his voice wasn't angry as much as bewil-dered. Chamika cringed and waited for the hammering she knew she deserved. But all she heard was his breathing, shallow and rapid, as if he'd run miles. Chamika relaxed and started to explain that she needed to start driving if she wanted to get home at a reasonable time. Christos interrupted her. "No, what you're going to do is you're come here to my house, *our* house, and I'm going to tell you the truth. I don't believe this sudden act of yours, Chamika. Now? After so much time you care? But you know, if any little part of you is sincere, then maybe yeah, you should hear the truth." She considered not going, but she knew Christos was right. She'd made a rum hash of things, coming to Vermont. She would have to see it through.

Christos ushered Chamika into the den and asked her to have a seat on the couch. He didn't sit. Instead he paced the length of the cof-fee table. He had his cell phone in one hand. A day's growth of beard covered his jaw. His clothes were disheveled and his eyes bloodshot. Christos told her that he was going to call Amanthi right there, so that Chamika could speak to her. But he wanted to explain his side first. His tone was drained of inflection or emotion, a man too tired to do anything else but explain the facts. He told Chamika he would never hurt Amanthi, especially not physically. Amanthi was the one who had left him. Three weeks before. But the separation wasn't final. Christos still had hope.

Christos had called Amanthi after Chamika had left and Amanthi had admitted that she had called her father for the money. She had wanted to believe, for a moment, that her father would be willing to help her. Christos sighed. That was the thing, wasn't it? Amanthi's family? Amanthi had long ago come to believe nobody in her family cared. Amanthi's family rarely called unless they needed something. The few times she asked for help, they ignored her. When Amanthi had stopped calling, when she had pretended to cut herself off hoping someone might notice and respond, she had received nothing, not even an email. Amanthi had been so depressed by her family's behavior it had effected their marriage. That was why no one returned Chamika's phone call. Christos had disconnected the phone not because of Chamika's call but because he couldn't stand explaining to Amanthi's friends who still didn't know she had left. And, he hadn't believed Chamika serious about wanting to speak to Amanthi. Amanthi had assumed years ago that Chamika had given up on their friendship.

Christos stopped in front of Chamika, head bowed. She tried to tell him not to worry, she was leaving and wouldn't bother them anymore, but he ignored her. He appeared consumed by the need to admit all that had happened. If Chamika was so interested in their lives then she should know he too had betrayed Amanthi. In a near monotone, he related how he had gone and made several dumb mistakes. And now Amanthi had just decided she wanted to start again. The number Chamika had shown him? Two zeroes were missing but it looked like the number of the account Amanthi had opened for herself before she left him. She wanted a clean break. Away from her family. Away from her husband. She wanted to be her own person. He repeated those three words. Her own person. Then, he closed his eyes and swayed. Chamika embarrassed that she had compelled this confession and afraid for him, that he might reveal even more to her, wanted only to distract him for a moment, to relieve him of the need to admit anything else to her.

She reached out and grabbed his elbow to steady him. His body collapsed at her touch. Christos was heavier than she expected, so much so that she was forced to stand and brace herself against his weight.

For a tumultuous moment, she thought they would both end up crashing into the coffee table but she didn't let go. Eventually, Christos regained his balance, and Chamika helped him to sit on the edge of the coffee table. She returned to the couch. He huddled, elbows propped on his thighs, face in hands. "I just want her to come back," he sobbed. "I love her."

"I can see that," Chamika replied sincerely. She held out her hand. She didn't want to. She wasn't the sort of person who comforted people by physical touch, but it seemed in that moment what he needed. Christos stared at the open palm as if not understanding at first what it meant. Eventually, he placed his hand in hers.

Christos sat breathing hard, clearly spent. Chamika held his hand in hers, forcing herself not to flinch or pull back. She couldn't predict everything that would happen. She couldn't promise Amanthi would come back. But Chamika knew from experience there would come a point when Amanthi realized escape was only the feeblest of protests. The act of closing herself off, of inuring herself to the loss of all she had left wasn't an indication of strength or willpower but a pretense, an indulgence. It was equally as weak to be the one to go, as it was to be the one who remained. It was as weak to cut someone off, as it was to be cut away.

Christos let go of Chamika's hand and started to punch numbers into the phone. Chamika heard the phone ring on the other end. A woman answered. The voice was familiar. Chamika hadn't realized until that moment how happy her cousin's voice would make her. Christos didn't answer the phone. Instead, he handed it to Chamika. She could hear Amanthi's voice repeating Christos's name, asking what he wanted.

Chamika took the phone and placed it against her ear. "It's not Christos," she said. Chamika heard the sharp intake of breath. "He called you because I asked him to," she explained. "I've been trying to reach you, nangi, and I'm here at your house."

"Who is this?" Amanthi demanded. "Is this a trick?"

"No trick. It's me," Chamika replied. The initial joy on hearing

Amanthi's voice was already fading. She had been foolish to pursue this, and she'd done so never truly anticipating this moment. Chamika would have to invent a suitable explanation for her silence. And what could she possibly say? Chamika had not cared fifteen years ago when it mattered about the harm she might cause. It struck her as meaningless to care so much now. "It's me, Chamika-akki." Amanthi still hadn't spoken. There was little chance that Chamika and Amanthi could right their friendship. All Chamika could hope to do was, by the sound of her voice, briefly put the lie to the fact no one had cared. But even that Chamika doubted. She had long ago forsaken any chance of having any such effect. "I'm very sorry," Chamika said. "I'm sorry about everything that has happened." Only silence. "I'm sorry, nangi, I waited too long to call."

ACKNOWLEDGMENTS

My sincere gratitude to the staff at University of Massachusetts Press, Laura Willwerth, and Jeff Parker for supporting this book and helping to shepherd it into the world. Many thanks to the Rona Jaffe Foundation for providing the support for the research and travel that this book required. Thank you also to the MacDowell Colony and Yaddo for providing me the time and physical space to work. I am endlessly grateful to many teachers for their wisdom and guidance: Sheila Kohler, Claire Messud, Sigrid Nunez, Linsey Abrams, and H. Aram Veeser. Dharshini Gunatilleke and Tamara Bernard offered me a home while in Colombo and the warmest and most generous of friendships. Harshini de Silva and Gayani Gamage have provided love and selfless guidance. Pamela Laskin, Matthew Pitt, Tomás Q. Morin, Marie Mutsuki Mockett, Steven Featherstone, Celeste Ng, and V. V. Ganeshananthan have given me their time, encouragement, and friendship, asking nothing in return. Brian Carroll continually inspires me with his deep intelligence and determination. Joel Holub read each story multiple times without complaint. I couldn't have accomplished this without him. This collection is his too. My family has been an unceasing source of love and encouragement. My Aunt Kashini for providing me a second home in Sri Lanka. Dulantha and Parker are the brothers I never had, until recently, but always wanted. I am so proud of my awesome and extraordinary sisters, Imali and Manoma. My biggest debt, though, is to my mother and my thaththa. They have modeled for me lives of bravery, kindness, and honesty. My respect and love runs deep and wide.

Thank you to the editors of the following magazines and anthologies where my work appeared:

"Third Country National," appeared in *Glimmer Train* and was named a distinguished story by *Best American Short Stories 2011*.

"War Wounds" appeared in *The Kenyon Review* and was named a distinguished story by *Best American Short Stories 2012*.

"Unicorn" appeared in *Skidrow Penthouse*.

"The Chief Inspector's Daughter" appeared in *StoryQuarterly* and *Narrative*.

"Ismail" appeared in *Narrative*.

"Pine" appeared in *Best New American Voices 2005*.

"The Inter-Continental" appeared in *Epoch*.

"The Demon" appeared in the *Bellevue Literary Review*.

"Treble Seven, Double Naught" appeared in *descant*.

A note: For the transliteration of all Sinhala and Tamil words I used as my guide either *The Postcolonial Identity of Sri Lankan English*, by Manique Gunesekera (University of Kelaniya, Sri Lanka, 2005), or *A Dictionary of Sri Lankan English*, by Michael Meyler (Mirisgala, 2007).

JUNIPER
JUNIPER PRIZE FOR FICTION

This volume is the eleventh recipient
of the Juniper Prize for Fiction,
established in 2004 by the
University of Massachusetts Press
in collaboration with the
UMass Amherst MFA Program
for Poets and Writers, to be
presented annually for an outstanding
work of literary fiction. Like its sister award,
the Juniper Prize for Poetry established
in 1976, the prize is named in honor
of Robert Francis (1901–1987),
who lived for many years at
Fort Juniper, Amherst, Massachusetts.